Advance Praise for
Hello Stars

"Lena in the Spotlight—*Hello Stars* is a bold and colorful story that will engage and inspire young readers. With a sturdy safety net of solid morals, Lena will encourage a generation of young women to shoot for the stars without compromising their dignity. The tween in your life will laugh with Lena and relate to her at the same time. Then, she'll beg you for the next book in the series!"

—PRISCILLA SHIRER,
Author and Bible teacher

"As an artist, inspiration is something I don't take for granted. It often comes through scripture, family, fellow artists, and recently, one of the sweetest 12-year-olds I've ever met. Alena's passion for serving the Lord and encouraging others is an inspiration to everyone she meets. I'm honored to know her and am excited about how this new series, Lena in the Spotlight, will inspire others."

—JAMIE-GRACE HARPER

"Tween girls LOVE fiction, but it doesn't always teach them the best values. That's why I'm so excited about Wynter Evans Pitts writing with her daughter Alena. This is a book that will entertain your daughter's love of reading, but also introduce godly living. Enjoy!"

—DANNAH GRESH

"Lena Daniels is like any other fifth-grade girl—only now she is a movie star. And she's spending the summer in LA with her favorite music artist. What starts as a dream come true leads Lena on an emotional rollercoaster, and as her life changes over-night, Lena is forced to change and rely heavily on God in a new unknown. This charming debut from a dynamic mother-daughter duo shares God's truth while addressing the quiet struggles of growing up and the self-doubt that emerges even in the best opportunities. Kudos to Lena and Wynter Pitts for creating a resource that gives girls an exciting behind-the-scenes peek at fame and illustrates what it means to shine the spotlight on God. I can't wait to share this book with my four daughters!"

—KARI KAMPAKIS, author of *Liked: Whose Approval Are You Living For?* and *10 Ultimate Truths Girls Should Know*

"Alena Pitts is an absolute treasure! She and her parents have a heart for ministry and for advancing God's kingdom. One of the best decisions we made in casting for the movie War Room was in choosing Alena to be Danielle. She not only brought an outstanding performance to the film, but she and her family were a joy to work with. We can look forward to great things from this little world changer."

—STEPHEN KENDRICK

Every little girl dreams and Alena Pitts has written a delightful book that will help any girl do just that. Taking a cue from her own life as a young actress, Alena weaves a story that will take her reader on a fun adventure while simultaneously encouraging her to both dream and keep first things first. The concepts of faith, family, and following your dreams are all laced together into a tale that is sure to keep any girl turning the pages while she also learns life lessons and is reminded of God's love.

—CHRYSTAL EVANS HURST, Co-author of *Kingdom Woman*

faithgirlz

LENA IN THE SPOTLIGHT

Hello Stars

HOLLYWOOD

BY ALENA PITTS
WITH WYNTER PITTS

ZONDERkidz™

ZONDERKIDZ

Hello Stars
Copyright © 2017 by Alena Pitts and Wynter Pitts
Illustrations © 2017 Zondervan

This title is also available as a Zondervan ebook.

Requests for information should be addressed to:
Zonderkidz, *3900 Sparks Dr. SE, Grand Rapids, Michigan 49546*

ISBN 978-0-310-76059-7

Cover Illustration: Annabelle Metayer
Interior Illustrations: Jacqui Davis
Interior design: Denise Froehlich

Printed in the United States of America

17 18 19 20 21 22 23 / LSC / 13 12 11 10 9 8 7 6 5 4 3 2 1

This is for Kaitlyn, Camryn, and Olivia.
I pray you always shine for Jesus—
you make our world brighter!

Chapter 1

"Mom, don't forget to let Austin out today," I yelled back through the two glass kitchen doors. Austin was still standing there, watching as Amber and I were the first to head out for the day.

I kept thinking about him and how badly I wished he could come to school with me. I once asked my science teacher, Mr. Lipscomb, if we could use him as a class pet but the idea was quickly rejected when he realized Austin doesn't like to sit still, partially follows rules, and sometimes nibbles on chairs. But how awesome would school be if he could be there? Totally awesome.

Oh, Austin is my wrinkle-faced, floppy eared, four-legged friend. Technically he's a blue-nosed bully puppy but he's much more human than any dog I have ever met.

"Just twenty-eight days left, boy!" I yelled louder to get him excited.

Dad flung the doors open with Ansley and Ashton hurrying behind him.

"Love you, Mom!"

Austin scurried away and my sisters and I followed Dad and headed to the van.

"Twenty-eight days till what, Lena?" Amber asked.

"That's how many days I have left in the fifth grade! Then it's summer vacation and I can't wait!"

Amber took the news and chased behind Dad calling his name until she reached his side.

She reached him right before he slid the back door open. She wrapped her tiny arms around his khaki pant leg and exclaimed, "It's almost summer!"

One-by-one we tossed our book bags, lunchboxes, and water bottles in and hopped into the back of our minivan.

"I wanted to tell you I have to go out of town today. It's a quick trip so I won't be home this evening, but I'll see you in time for school tomorrow morning, ok?"

"Ok!" we responded in unison.

Ansley used the short car ride to school to discuss her upcoming ninth birthday plans, while Ashton and Amber sat in the back talking about how excited they were to be graduating from kindergarten in just a few weeks.

"Ok, here we are." Dad's announcement caused everyone to pause their conversations.

I glanced down at my watch. The digits 8:12 flashed before my eyes.

"We only have three minutes! I don't want to be late today."

Dad pulled his car forward until we reached the main school doors. They were already swinging shut.

Dad let out a deep grunt. "Sorry guys. Love you!"

"Love you too, Daddy!" we yelled as we hopped out of the van and headed into the big brick building.

Ansley ran to the left, Amber and Ashton to the right, and I raced straight ahead to Ms. Blount's history class. I whispered a silent prayer, *"Dear God, please let her door still be open."*

I hated being late to Ms. Blount's class. She's my history and language arts teacher. She also happens to be a huge rule follower. So if her door was closed then I would most definitely need to get a tardy pass from the office. Which meant that I would be even later to class than I already was.

Unfortunately, when I reached room 109, the door was closed.

I carefully stood on my tiptoes to peek through the skinny glass window next to the door. I wanted to see inside without Ms. Blount seeing or hearing me. Everyone was shuffling around in their backpacks and shoving loose papers into their notebooks. I waited until my eyes met Savannah's. She flashed a sheepish grin in my direction and quickly looked away.

Savannah is always on time and prepared. I remember meeting her in the first grade. When I walked into the classroom she was sitting straight against the back of her chair, her feet placed perfectly side-by-side in front her, and she had on a pair of white ruffled socks that matched the two large white hair bows dangling from each side of her head. Her hands were crossed delicately, resting on top of her desk. She looked perfect and I knew right away we would become the best of friends.

I dropped back down to my heels and exhaled. I marched to the office and filled out the tardy sheet. I crumbled the pink copy with the faded words and stuffed it into my backpack. I balled the white copy up in my left fist and marched right back up to room 109. I knocked on the door, held up the crinkled copy of the white excuse sheet and smiled. Ms. Blount opened the door and welcomed me in.

"Good morning, Ms. Blount," I said apologetically.

"Good morning," she replied without ever moving her actual mouth. I'm always amazed at how she does that. No expression. No smile. No eye contact. Just a gravelly voice that escapes a tiny hole between her top and bottom lips.

I handed her the paper as quickly as I could and slid past her through the door and into the room. I spotted my empty chair right next to Savannah, so I headed in that direction to take my place.

As I walked past Savannah's desk, I nodded and mouthed, "How'd it go?" She knew I was talking about her weekend at our favorite singer Mallory Winston's concert, so she gave me a *can't wait to tell you about it, but not now* thumbs up and finished coloring in the pattern of funny faces she had already drawn all over her worksheet.

Great, I thought to myself.

Ms. Blount was in the middle of explaining how George Washington had never really cut down a cherry tree.

I put on my glasses, opened my eyes really wide, and tried to focus.

For some reason it wasn't working. I just couldn't seem to stop my brain from drifting into a magical world full of baby Austins swimming in pools of cherry flavored whipped cream clouds surrounded by rainbows and puppy treats.

Before I knew it, half the day was over and everyone was grabbing their things and heading to lunch.

"I'm starving! Let's find Emma," Savannah announced as we strolled toward the cafeteria.

Savannah and I scanned the large room until we spotted

Emma in the middle of a huge crowd. She was wearing her knee-high white lace socks, her navy uniform skirt with the two large red buttons on the front, and she had her black fringed vest tossed on over her white uniform shirt.

Emma burst through the crowd chanting, "Lena! Lena! Savannah! Hey, over here!"

"Hey, girl!" Savannah wrapped her arms around Emma's neck. "Love the socks."

"Me too. But wait until Ms. Blount sees them! You're gonna get it!" I sneered playfully.

"Wait—what's wrong with these?" Emma seemed genuinely surprised by my warning as she knocked her knees together and shrugged innocently.

I have never been able to figure out how she can get away with being completely out of uniform every day, but she does. It's probably because Emma knows how to make everyone smile with her silly jokes and spunky smile. She is always ready to have fun and I think even the overly strict teachers like Ms. Blount appreciate that.

Savannah and I followed Emma to a table mostly full of friends from her homeroom. This is the first year since first grade that the three of us haven't shared a single class together. We missed her but our friendship is strong enough to survive a few hours apart.

Emma slid into the open space between two of her friends while Savannah and I sat directly across from them. Deliberately and quietly everyone emptied their lunch bags. I reached into my right pocket and pulled out my sandwich. Then I reached into my left and grabbed a handful of snacks.

"Still no lunchbox?" Savannah asked

"Nope, and I'm not ready to tell my mom yet. Anyone want my fruit snacks?" I waved the little blue bag from side-to-side in the air.

"Oooo, I'll take them!" Emma reached across the table to grab them but I pulled them back just in time for her hand to land on top of my already smooshed sandwich. We all burst out laughing.

I put my finger over my open mouth and whispered "shhh," through my giggles. I could feel Ms. Blount glaring in our direction and I didn't want anyone to get in trouble.

"Hurry and eat guys, so we can go outside. We have a lot to talk about!" Savannah urged.

"Oooo, I almost forgot!" Emma practically screamed.

"You went to Mallory Winston's concert! Did you get to meet her? Which songs did she sing?" Emma tossed question after question out to Savannah. Savannah caught each of them and calculated her thoughts before offering any responses. Emma and I were sitting on the edge of our seats filled with anticipation.

Savannah's grandmother had given her two tickets for her birthday. Emma and I were pretty sad that we didn't get to go with her but we didn't think it would be fair for her to choose just one of us, so we all agreed it would be best if she took her cousin instead. At least one of us got to go. All we needed was for her to tell us all about it!

"She'll fill us in after lunch," I said quietly to try and calm Emma down a bit.

I could see Ms. Blount moving toward our table.

"Uh-oh."

Her steps were long and slow until she was standing

in the small space between my back and the fourth grade table behind me.

I stuffed a few green grapes into my mouth. Savannah took a gulp from her orange water bottle while Emma continued to talk.

"Savannah, I can't wait! Please tell me now!"

"Lena Daniels," Ms. Blount spoke sternly.

I wasn't even talking, I thought to myself.

I spun around but in slow motion.

"Yes, ma'am?" I whimpered in a voice of total fear and complete panic.

"Mr. Lipscomb would like to see you in the science room," she said. "Finish your lunch and go straight there. You can head right to recess after."

I said a quick "yes, ma'am," and turned back around. I took the last bite of my sandwich and jumped up from the table.

"Don't say anything about Mallory until I get back!"

I doubled my normal walking speed as I headed to Mr. Lipscomb's room.

He greeted me at the door and his first words were, "Tomorrow is dissection day—"

From there, I knew exactly what he wanted. Mr. Lipscomb always calls on me when he needs help in the science lab. He says I am responsible. He wanted me to clean the tables before the dissection the next day. I asked him why we cleaned the tables before if it was just going to get covered in slime, blood, and animal guts. He said it needed to be sanitary for the animals. I didn't understand this either. Why do we make it sanitary for a *dead* animal?

I am 99% sure the animal doesn't have feelings. And if it did, I'm pretty sure he or she was going to care a lot more about getting cut open and pulled apart than the table being cleaned for its second death.

But, oh well. I finished our conversation with "yes, sir, I can do it" and headed to recess.

Emma and Savannah ran toward me. "Lena! Lena! Hurry up!!!" they yelled.

Savannah did not waste any time before jumping right into all the fascinating Mallory Winston details we had been waiting to hear all morning.

"The concert was fabulous!"

Emma raised her hands in the air and wiggled her wrists, causing her hands to flail uncontrollably.

Savannah continued, "She was wearing purple boots! And she had a purple feather in her hair to match!"

"That's so cool!" Emma screeched.

"I want a pair," I said softly.

I am pretty sure Savannah didn't hear either of us. She was so excited that she just kept right on talking. It was so fun seeing her this energetic and full of spunk. Not many things can pull this much enthusiasm from Savannah but Mallory Winston had a way of making us all smile.

"When she first came on stage she was alone with just one tiny light shining on her. She was holding her guitar and guess what she sang?" Savannah asked but we all knew she didn't need an answer.

She had our full attention. We stood directly in front of her, captivated by each word she spoke.

"Lena, she sang "Run Away with Me"!"

I bent my knees and pushed my body downward playfully until I was almost on the ground.

Savannah reached down and pretended to catch me. "Don't worry. We recorded it for you. I'll show you the next time you come over!"

"Yay!" I cheered.

Savannah's eyes grew as big as ping-pong balls and she leaned forward. "You guys are not going to believe this . . . it's the best part—Mallory Winston is having a contest! It's like a chance to audition for a movie. But guess what the best part is?"

"What??" The anticipation was building and I could feel my heart doing a happy dance inside my chest.

"The winner will get to meet her! You and Emma have to do it! This is your chance to meet Mallory Winston!"

The three of us became one big ball of bouncy noise.

"Wait, but how?" Emma said exactly what I was thinking.

"She said the information is on her website. Just go to it and enter!"

We all jumped up and down again.

"Savannah, you have to do it too!" I demanded even though I already knew she probably wouldn't. She's way too shy for that.

The bell rang and we darted in separate directions.

"Bye, Emma!" Savannah and I called as we headed inside and back towards Room 109.

When Ms. Blount announced we had earned a little reward time for finishing our grammar worksheets on time, I knew exactly what I wanted to do. I needed to tell someone about my chance to meet Mallory! I found the huge blue beanbag in the back corner of our classroom under the huge wooden frame we made as a class. It looked like a window full of stars in the middle of the wall. We'd each signed our names on a little star and placed them on a huge piece of dark blue construction paper behind the frame. Ms. Blount said she wanted us to always remember to shine.

I opened the little black notebook I had recently gotten for my eleventh birthday, and started writing.

Hello, Stars,

Today is the best day ever! You know that Mallory Winston concert that Savannah went to? Well, she just told us all about it and that there's a chance I could actually meet her!! That would be the best thing ever! I'm gonna pray and ask God to make that happen. Mallory loves God and I love her, so I hope He listens!

Dear God,

Can you help me to meet Mallory Winston? Ok, thanks!

For the rest of the day my head was spinning with the thought of meeting Mallory Winston. Even though I had no idea what I needed to do, I was determined that I would do it as soon as I got home.

Chapter 2

The sound of the last bell tickled my ears. I gathered all of my things and raced to the van. Mom hit the little button when she saw me coming and by the time I reached the door it was already open. I plopped right in, ignoring my sisters, and started talking, "Mom, you are not going to believe what Savannah told me today!"

"Oh really? What is it?" Mom kept her eyes on the road in front of her but she made sure I could see her smile through the rearview mirror.

"You know how Savannah went to Mallory Winston's concert this weekend?"

Mom nodded.

"Well, she said Mallory told everyone she's having a contest and that the winner would have a chance to meet her and audition to be in a movie with her!" My mouth was moving fast and the words were spilling out.

"Oh wow, Lena. That's great," Mom said.

"Wait, how Lena?" Ansley asked.

"Well, I don't know all the details yet, but I wanted to know if I can enter when we get home. Can I, Mom?"

"We can certainly talk about it."

"Mom! Please!" I begged.

"First we'll need to know what the contest is and what you have to do." At a stoplight Mom reached her hand back and quickly patted my leg to try and calm my excitement.

"I know," I said quickly. "Savannah says that all the details are on her website."

"Ok, let's take a look when we get home. After homework of course."

"Yes! Of course."

I sat back in my seat smiling from ear to ear, picturing what it would be like to actually meet Mallory Winston. Mom knows how much I love her. She's the one who got me her CD for my tenth birthday and I have loved her ever since.

I spent the rest of the car ride trying to explain to Ashton that Savannah said this was for big girls only and even though she was a big girl she wasn't big *enough* yet. I promised that I would take everyone with me if I won.

"So if you meet her, then we will get to meet her too right, Lena?" Ashton confirmed.

"Yes." I nodded. "Absolutely."

I smiled back at her toothless six-year old grin.

The car had barely come to a stop before I hopped out and ran into the playroom to get to work on my homework.

After finishing, I grabbed my mom's computer and typed www.mallorywinston.com.

"Calling all girls 10–12 years old!" was highlighted across the top of the page in flashing black letters. I scrolled the little black arrow directly on top of the words and waited anxiously as a video loaded.

"Hey! So I have a little bit of fun for you girls." There she was—Mallory.

"I'm gonna be in a movie. Like a for real movie! Now I know what you are thinking—*Mallory, you are not an actress*—and I agree! Crazy right? But here is the thing.

You are right, I am not an actress. But I am God's girl and that means I'll do whatever He tells me to do! This movie is an awesome opportunity to shine God's love on the world so I am doing it! And guess what?"

"What?" I replied back as if she could hear me.

"I want you to do it with me! We are looking for a girl between the ages of ten and twelve years old to be in the movie with me! The best part is, you don't need to be actress either. You just need to send me a video telling me who you are and why you want to audition and anything else random and cool that you want me to know!"

Mallory's video message ended with, "Just do it and see what happens. Remember, anything is possible with Jesus. He loves you and has a big plan for your life!"

"Well . . ." Mom's words startled me. I was so intrigued with Mallory and her announcement that I hadn't even heard her come into the room.

"Can I do it?" I asked.

Mom's forehead had three tiny wrinkles forming in the space where her eyes meet her nose. "Lena, do you realize it's for a chance to audition for a movie? You would meet Mallory but that's not really what the contest is for. Do you even want to be in a movie?"

I paused for a moment. "Like be an actress?" I could feel my forehead creasing, mirroring my mother's.

I had never actually thought about it. My sisters and I loved to make up plays and shows. Sometimes we even recorded them and added cool music and effects. But this was also a chance to meet Mallory, so of course I wanted to do it.

"Well, yes. I'm sure I want to do it." Each word I spoke was a little more convincing than the one before it. "Even Mallory said you don't need to be a real actress, so why not? I mean I at least need to send a video, right?"

Mom looked at me as if she was trying to see inside my brain.

I stood tall and spoke loudly, "Yes! Yes, I want to be an actress!"

Mom dropped her mouth open and let out a high-pitched, "Ahhh, Lena."

"Is that a yes? Mommy, please? Can we record a video and send it to Mallory? Can we do it now? Please!"

"Ok, Lena."

"YES!!! I'm going to meet Mallory Winston!"

"Don't you mean you are going to enter the contest to *audition* for a part in a movie that Mallory Winston will be in?" Mom chuckled.

"Oh right . . . that's what I meant!"

I ran off and immediately scouted the house for a plain white wall and a quiet space to record in. The wall was way easier to find than the silence I needed. But after begging Ashton, Amber, and Ansley, they agreed to sit quietly and watch if I agreed to mention them in the video.

We had a deal.

"Mom, I'm ready! Bring your phone, please!"

I shoved a few fruit snacks into my mouth to try to calm my jittery stomach and waited as mom shuffled her way down the hall.

"Are you sure you are ready?" she asked. "Have you prepared anything?"

"Yup. I'm ready!"

"Do you know you have jelly on your shirt?" she laughed.

"Oh, that's weird. Must be from lunch. Stay here, I'll go change!"

I replaced my dingy uniform shirt with a fresh yellow T-shirt. I stood in front of the mirror, patted my hair down, and gave myself the once over before determining I was all ready.

Ashton stopped me in the hall and locked eyes with my khaki uniform skirt.

"It's fine. Mom will only record from the waist up," I assured her before she could voice her concern out loud.

"Mom, I'm ready."

Mom looked me over and gave me a thumbs up before hitting record. I leaned against the wall and stared directly into the little hole at the top of her phone. In two and a half minutes I told Mallory all about my life and my plans to be an Olympic swimmer and a volleyball player. I told her about Savannah and Emma and I told her to keep an eye out for their videos as well. As promised, I talked about each of my sisters. I told her how fun it was to have twin sisters and how opposite they are—

"Amber is so silly and Ashton is so serious! They are hilarious together. But then there is my other sister, Ansley. Ansley just makes us laugh all the time. She doesn't even try, and that's what so funny about her!"

When I finished talking, Mom handed me the phone to check the video.

"I'll watch it later," I told her and instead I immediately attached the file to an email and hit send.

Without giving Mom a chance to respond, I grabbed both of Mom's hands and forced her to dance in a circle with me while squealing, "We did it! Thank you, Mommy!"

For the rest of the evening my body felt like I had little ants crawling up and down my legs and I needed to keep shaking them off! So I did. I danced through dinner, had a personal concert in the shower, and slid up and down the halls in my stockinged feet until it was bedtime.

When Mom turned Ansley's and my bedroom light off for the night I was still singing. I was wide awake. My body was exhausted but when I closed my eyes I pictured myself standing next to Mallory wearing matching purple boots. "Can you sing one of my songs?" she'd ask. And of course I would belt out a beautiful array of her music until eventually she'd join me. We'd sing for hours, wear matching outfits, and live happily ever after.

My thoughts made me giggle.

"Ansley?" I whispered.

A grunt, moan, and snort were her reply.

"Ahhhh, I need to empty my brain."

I reached under my bed and grabbed my little book and pulled out my favorite "I Love Paris" pen. Then I scooted to the corner of my bed, right under my window. I knew just where to crawl in order to let the nighttime light hit the pages of my journal. I glanced up at the sky and smiled at the stars.

"Hello, stars," I whispered.

Hello, Stars.

It's me Lena, again. I know we just talked earlier but I promise I'll leave you alone after this. Ok, well except for my daily countdown to summer vacation, which by the way is only 27!

Remember I told you about the chance to meet Mallory? Well I did my part and I'm pretty sure it's going to happen. I'm going to meet Mallory Winston. Mom wants me to stop saying that and to say that I entered into a contest for chance to audition for a part in a movie . . . but that's way too complicated! I know it's not guaranteed but I have a feeling in my toes. I AM GOING TO MEET MALLORY WINSTON and I can't wait!! It's going to be fantastic!

OH YEAH!!!!!!!!!

And now . . . goodnight.

Chapter 3

"Lena, wake up." I could hear the words rattling in my brain but my body refused to respond.

"Lena, Daddy's getting us donuts!"

I opened my eyes and could see straight up Ansley's nose. She was standing so close I had to move just to see the rest of her face.

I rolled away from my sister's morning-breath greeting and sat straight up.

"Donuts?" I asked. And with one nod of her head, I was suddenly wide awake. I began to unravel my blanket from around my neck, pulling and pulling until I was finally able to break free.

"Come on, guys. Donuts today!" I hollered down the hall toward Ashton and Amber's room while headed for the bathroom.

"We already know!" their tiny voices called.

"Good morning, Mommy. I have to help Mr. Lipscomb today!" I bellowed down the hall.

"Hi, Lena." Dad poked his head in the bathroom. "We will be sure to get you there on time."

"Oh, hi, Daddy. Glad you're back!" I smiled.

"I can't wait to see this video! I've heard all about it!"

His words made my toes curl.

Within fifteen minutes I was fully dressed, my teeth

were brushed, and I was standing in the middle of the kitchen searching frantically for my lunchbox.

"Ash, Am, Ans—have you guys seen my lunchbox?"

"Nope."

"Nope."

"Nope."

"Urghhh," I moaned.

Please God, help me find it, I thought to myself.

Just as I was stuffing a peanut butter and honey sandwich into the side pocket of my polka-dot jacket, I was abruptly interrupted by a wet smack on my knee.

"Hey buddy, hold on." I reached down to pat Austin on the head and was met by his cold wet tongue instead.

"Ew!" I placed a hand behind each of his floppy ears and leaned down close to his navy blue nose, "Twenty seven days left, boy! Then I'm all yours for the summer!"

Austin scurried behind me, nibbling on the back of my shoes and circling my ankles until Dad announced that it was time to go.

Like almost always, we gathered around the back door to pray first. Ashton held out her tiny hand and linked with Amber. Amber locked elbows with Ansley while Ansley fumbled her backpack to the floor with her loose arm. I grabbed it and playfully squeezed my hand down her arm until our hands met. Mom rested one arm around my shoulder and the other around the bottom of Dad's waist. Dad left one arm free and held Mom's phone in his palm.

Standing like this, in a circle and attached to my family, is one of my favorite parts of the morning. I suppose it's like a family tradition. My Dad's mom prayed with him every morning and now he prays with us. It always reminds me of a team and this is our huddle before the game. Teams come up with a plan to take care of each other and work together in order to win. You never break a huddle and start playing knowing that your teammate isn't prepared. No one would start the game if a team member was wearing the wrong colored jersey or if their shoe was untied . . . team members take care of each other.

Dad says that prayer and God's Word give us our daily instructions. No one is ready for the day until we've read it together.

I closed my eyes and prepared to listen to my dad.

"Lena," he spoke. "Before we pray today, let's hear about this Mallory Winston contest!"

"Da—" was the only sound I could get out before Ansley interrupted.

'Let's watch the video!"

"Oh yeah!" I agreed. "I haven't even watched it yet!"

Standing even closer than we were before, giggling and squirming, we glued our eyes to the tiny screen resting in Dad's hand.

"OH NO!!!!!!" I screamed out immediately.

Everyone gasped.

There I was on the screen with a huge glob of gummy goo nesting between my top two front teeth.

"Why didn't anyone tell me my teeth were red?" I let out a desperate cry. Immediately I could feel tears welling in the bottom lids of my eyes.

Everyone remained silent and the look on my sisters'

faces was a mix of fear and total confusion. Their eyes were full of concern as a stream of tears poured down my face.

"What is that?" Dad was puzzled.

"Fruit snacks," Ashton answered for me.

"Is this the one you sent in?" he asked.

Mom tried to quiet his questions and resolve my meltdown. "It's ok, sweetie."

But it wasn't. The video had been sent.

"No, it's not! This is terrible!"

"Sorry, Lena. But don't worry about it." Dad took a concerned tone and began searching for something on Mom's phone.

He found what he was looking for and read, "Philippians 4:6 'Don't worry about anything, but in everything, through prayer and petition with thanksgiving, let your requests be made known to God'."

I stood in the middle of our family huddle and sobbed.

"How can I be thankful for this? This is terrible! I know that Mallory is laughing at my pathetic attempt to convince her that I am the one she should choose. How could she even take me seriously with a giant piece of fruit snack on my tooth?"

I sobbed even louder.

Mom hushed me with a full-body squeeze. I felt my body collapse into hers while a group of tiny fingers patted my back.

Mom spoke softly, "Lena, God isn't saying to be thankful because you made a mistake. He wants you to be thankful even though you made a mistake. See, God wants us to acknowledge His goodness in our lives even when things aren't going the way we want. He tells us not to worry about anything, even our mistakes, but to thank Him instead for His goodness and trust Him with everything. Even the things we think are mistakes. He can handle those if we ask Him to."

"Huh?" Ashton stole the words right from my mouth.

"God is compassionate to us. So He is not happy to see you so sad. But Lena, it really will be ok. Instead of focusing on the fruit snack, let's thank God for Mallory and the great opportunity this is. Then let's just trust Him for the plan He has for your life. Ok? Let's pray."

Mom released her squeeze just enough for Dad to place his hand on the side of my dripping wet face.

"Can I pray?" Amber asked.

Dad nodded.

"Dear God, thank you for this day and thank you that we are going to get donuts. I pray that you help Lena not be sad about her tooth and that you let Mallory pick her anyway. And that we all get to meet her. Amen."

"Amen."

When my eyes opened Mom was staring at me. "It's going to be ok, Lena!" Mom definitely had no way of knowing that it would be ok, but hearing her say those words did make me feel better.

"We need to head out for donuts if you plan to get to school on time today! Don't you have some dissection tables to clean?" Mom's voice was gentle and playful.

"Oh right! Guess we need to go," I said.

We hustled out the door, loaded up in the minivan, and headed straight for donuts. Dad did his best to distract me by telling us all about the time he worked all summer delivering newspapers because he needed to save enough money to buy a pair of red Chuck Taylors. However, when he wore them to school the first time everyone laughed at him and said his feet looked like two big water balloons!

His story did make me chuckle and Amber and Ashton laughed so hard their bellies started to hurt.

We arrived at school nice and early and I headed straight to the lab to clean the soon-to-be extra gross dissection tables. I wasn't in the mood but I knew Mr. Lipscomb was counting on me.

I opened the door to his room and immediately tripped over a squishy yellow bundle of chirping down.

"Ooooooh no." This could not be good.

Two weeks ago Mr. Lipscomb purchased baby chicks for our class. He also purchased a cage for them so I had no idea why they were scurrying around the classroom.

I flicked on the light and there they were—two of our new class pets. One was pecking around aimlessly and the other was doing something that involved smelling or looking at his chick friend's tail end.

Whatever he was doing seemed gross and I preferred not to stare. We had learned as a class that this is perfectly normal chick behavior. Now, there they were loose in the middle of our gigantic science lab. The lab I was supposed to clean before our big dissection today.

It finally sunk in that it was just me, the chicks, and this wide-open space. If anyone was going to do something, it had to be me.

I immediately went into full on Lena-to-the-rescue

mode. Sprinting from one corner of the room to the next panicking and chanting, "Oh no. Oh no. Gloves. Gloves. Oh no. Where are the gloves?"

I knew I needed to get those chicks back into their cage before they tried to eat the frozen frogs that were lying in crates on the floor. Do chicks even eat frogs? I had no idea, but I knew this could not be good.

I needed to find the gloves. The last thing I wanted to do was touch a tail-sniffing chick without gloves on.

"Found them!" I shouted to myself.

I grabbed the box of rubber gloves and tried to pull one out. After frantically tugging at them for about six seconds, I ended up with about nine gloves in my hand and twenty-five more all over the floor.

"I'll worry about those later," I said out loud.

I kept one eye on the escapees while heading toward the cage. Mr. Lipscomb bought eight chicks and I needed to make sure the other six were where they were supposed to be.

I peeked in the cage and gasped!

The remaining chicks were stepping on top of each other, flapping their little wings, and using their food bowl as a ladder. They were all trying to escape!

"Oh no ya don't! Nice try," I mumbled. "Great teamwork, guys," I had to admit.

I reached down just in time to catch the third escapee midflight and dropped him back into the cage with the rest of them. His sudden return caused them all to disperse a bit and delayed their plans.

I, on the other hand, needed a plan. And I needed one quick.

I scanned the room for a lid for the cage or something that I could use as a temporary top. I found NOTHING . . . absolutely NOTHING.

"Think, Lena, think," I said to myself.

"Uhhhh-ahhh!" I remembered I was wearing a jacket. I immediately slid it off, tied a sleeve to opposite sides of the cage, covering as much of the top as I could.

By now the two original escapees had wandered all the way to the back of the room, and were under Mr. Lipscomb's desk. I trotted over to them, caught one, and ran it back to the cage. I raced back for the other, grabbed him, and dropped him in as well.

I was two seconds away from breathing a sigh of relief when I felt something tickling my ankle.

Another one had escaped. This one must have been smart and quick because he found the one open space near my jacket collar and flapped his new wings right through it.

"1, 2, 3, 4, 5, 6, 7 . . . oh no!"

Another had escaped.

I chased him down and turned to drop him back in only to find that now there were only three chicks in the cage. The jacket was dangling off one corner by a sleeve. These chicks were impossible to catch! Every time I placed one back in, another had already used his friends' backs to hop out.

This entire incident was going downhill really fast. I reached down and tried to grab as many as I could in one swift scoop. Just as I was wrapping my arms around the bundle of chicks, in walked Savannah and Emma.

I immediately dropped them all. The chicks made a thump when they landed and scattered across the entire floor. Flapping, chirping, and sniffing.

This was not good.

Savannah's face turned tomato red and she opened her mouth wide as if she wanted to scream but nothing came out. Just one big gasp.

"Come on, Savannah! Help!" Emma screeched as she bent down and tried to help me capture the fleeing birds.

Seconds later Mr. Lipscomb walked in and froze with one foot in the door and the other midair while he screamed, "Lena! Emma! Savannah! What is happening in here?"

"We didn't do it!" I protested, realizing we were the only students in the room and unlike Savannah and Emma I was covered in fuzz.

Mr. Lipscomb began chasing the chicks across the room. "Get to class, girls!" he snapped. "I'll take care of this and deal with you later."

The urgency in his voice demanded our instant obedience and in a single file line we quickly marched out.

"Lena, who let the chicks out?" Emma asked.

"I have no idea! They were out when I walked in."

"Wow, sorry we didn't show up sooner." Savannah's apology was sincere.

"I'm so glad you came to help. There is no way I could have caught them by myself. Wait, why did you come in there anyway?"

Emma did a full body spin and skipped backwards.

"Well, we wanted to know if you sent a video to Mallory and we knew you'd be here early today!"

My heart dropped and I immediately felt the urge to hold back tears. Fighting the runaway chicks had actually taken my mind off the gummy goo.

"Oh yeah, well, yeah. Sort of."

"Ok, tell us later. We need to get to class before Ms. Blount closes the door! Emma, see ya at lunch!" Savannah pulled me in the same direction while gently shoving Emma toward her part of the long skinny corridor.

We dashed down the hall and slipped through the still slightly open door of the classroom just in time.

"Good morning, class." Ms. Blount shut the door behind us.

While I waited for her to start the day I sat quietly with my pen, paper, and little notebook in hand and pretended to be invisible.

Oh, Stars,

I wonder how long it will be before the news about the chicks spreads. Mr. Lipscomb is going to tell Ms. Blount. Ms. Blount is going to tell the principal, and the principal will call my mom. Mom will call Dad and Dad will show up at the school, call me to the office, and demand an explanation. Someone from my class will see my dad come into the office and create an elaborate story about Emma,

Savannah, and me getting into a fight in the science lab, knocking over the chicken coup, and being sent to the office by Ms. Blount for causing such a commotion . . . can this day get any worse? I'm trying not to worry here but clearly it's not working! I wish I could just disappear!

Chapter 4

I waited the entire day for the chick scenario to play out. Strangely, Mr. Lipscomb didn't say a word during science class and by recess my palms were sweaty, my heart was pounding, and my eyes were tired from holding back tears all morning. I tried to hide them from Emma and Savannah but I couldn't. My eyelashes were already wet when we headed out the cafeteria doors for recess.

"Lena, they're just chicks. Not a big deal. Mr. Lipscomb doesn't even seem upset anymore. Besides, we have your back!" Emma did some sort of a tribal dance routine to try cheering me up.

Savannah laughed extra hard and eventually I cracked a smile.

"Guys, it's not just the chicks." I paused. Did I really want to tell them about my Mallory Winston video?

I decided I wasn't ready yet. "I've just had a really terrible morning."

"Group hug!" Emma threw her hands around our shoulders and leaned forward until she was mostly in the middle of our little circle.

"So, my mom wouldn't let me send a video to Mallory," Emma announced. "She says trying to be in a movie would be way too much work and maybe we can just buy passes to meet her the next time she's in town. How about yours, Lena?"

I dropped my eyes to the ground and spoke casually, "Oh yeah, I sent it but I probably won't win. It was really terrible. I'm actually hoping Mallory never sees it. The passes are a much better idea."

"Yeah, let's try to do that!" Savannah was easily convinced and for a few seconds Emma seemed happy enough with my short explanation until she thought about it a little more.

"Wait, Lena. What was wrong with your video?" she prodded.

I responded quickly and tried to avoid eye contact, "It was just bad. Had something in my teeth."

Surprisingly, neither Emma nor Savannah laughed. I was starting to feel like maybe the gooey teeth weren't that bad. Emma smacked her lips dramatically while Savannah gave me a sympathetic smile.

By the time the bell rang at the end of the day, I was mentally exhausted.

I spotted my mom's van in the carpool line and dragged my tired body directly to her.

"Lena!" My mom was practically hanging out the window yelling my name from the moment she saw me coming.

When I sank into my seat, so did my heart. I felt like my entire day was sitting at the bottom of my stomach.

"Lena! Mallory Winston emailed you! Can you believe it? Already!" she screamed. Without taking a break for air she continued, "Lena, she loved your video and gave it to the directors of the movie! They want you to audition! LENA? Did you hear me?"

I sat silently. I was completely frazzled and totally confused.

She spoke louder this time. I could hear my sisters giggling but everything sounded muffled like it was coming through a very long skinny tunnel.

"MALLORY WINSTON emailed . . . you . . . me . . . the directors want . . ."

I burst into tears.

Apparently this was not the response my mother was expecting because she decided to repeat the entire thing.

This time I cried even harder. Nothing she was saying made any sense, and all I could think about was how frustrating the entire day had been.

Finally she stopped saying Mallory's name and asked, "What is wrong, Lena?"

At that moment everything I had been holding in for the last seven hours came flooding out of my eyes and I could not control it. I told Mom all about the run-away chicks, reminded her of my gummy video disaster, and even confessed that I'd lost my lunchbox and had been eating my lunch out of my pockets.

My mother kept her eyes on the road but her eyebrows were wrinkled in a frown. The right side of her bottom lip was tucked under her top two big teeth. But she didn't say a word, she just let me talk it out. Amber and Ashton's eyes were as big as golf balls as I continued to weep.

Ansley broke the silence with, "Lena, you never found your lunchbox?"

Instantly my emotional breakdown turned into a hysterical uproar! Everyone was afraid to laugh but not even I could hold it in. Ansley was so genuine with her concern and after everything I had just confessed, all she was worried about was the fact that I still couldn't find my lunchbox!

We laughed until we were all in tears. As the giggles started to simmer down, my mom turned slightly to me and said, "Well, it's nice to see you smiling again!"

"Hey Mom, what did you say about Mallory Winston?" I squeaked.

Ansley, Amber, and Ashton joined me and we listened to Mom retell about the email, and just that quickly I forgot all about my emotional breakdown.

The rest of the evening was one big celebration including ice cream, movies, and giggles. When it was finally bedtime I knew I wouldn't be able to sleep. I waited patiently for Ansley to whisper her last words before grabbing my little black book and slipping into my closet for a little alone time.

HELLLLLOOOO!!!!!!!!!!!!!! STARS!!!!

Today was such a weird day. This morning I really thought my life was over. I felt awful after the Mallory Winston disaster video and then the whole chick scenario. That was all so crazy. I'm so glad Emma and Savannah were there to help even though it didn't really help. At least I wasn't alone. I would not have survived this day without them and now look at how everything has changed! No one found out or teased me about the chicks and Mallory actually picked my video even with the gummy mouth! I'm almost too embarrassed to meet her now . . . well no, not really, but I do wish that my video had been better. Anyway, I spent all that time stressing and crying for nothing. I feel so silly. I guess Dad was right. I need to stop worrying about things and let God handle it! This is crazy . . . I may really get to meet Mallory Winston after all!!

Mallory Winston emailed me!

Thank you, God!!

Chapter 5

"Hello," I could hear Mom answering her phone in the short distance between my bedroom door and hers. My ears perked up and I lay very still, hoping to catch any details of her conversation. I didn't want to be nosey, I only listened long enough to realize the voice on the other end was not Mallory Winston and the conversation had nothing to do with me or my recent video audition.

I rolled over and planted my face into the palms of my hands. "Why won't they call?" I mumbled into my pillow.

I glanced up at the square calendar above my desk. It had been weeks since I sent in the video audition for the part in *Above the Waters* and we still had not heard anything from Mallory, the director people, or anyone else.

I could feel my heart starting to ache. I'm not sure if I really wanted to be in the movie or if it just hurt my feelings to know they hadn't chosen me. It was becoming harder and harder to not let the suspense and anticipated disappointment take over.

"Lena? Are you ok?" Ansley sat up in her bed and stared in my direction.

I forced an excited tone into my words, "Yup, sorry for waking you up." Then I dragged myself across the room and plopped, elbows first, at the edge of her bed.

"Happy Birthday!!!!!!" I shouted while smothering her with a huge hug and numerous kisses!

She giggled and melted forward into the pile of blankets nestled at her feet.

"Lena, stop!" she chuckled as I continued to tickle her.

After catching her breath and letting a few last giggles escape, she asked, "Were you just crying?"

"Well," I paused and tried to perk up a little more. I didn't want to ruin Ansley's birthday joy. "I'm just a little sad that I have not heard back from Mallory or the Fenway Production people. It's been so long and I don't think I got the part. I really wanted it though."

"It's ok, Lena. Remember what Mommy was telling us last night?"

I nodded and looked away. I knew exactly what Ansley was talking about and I didn't want to talk about it again. I really just wanted the phone to ring and for it to be Mallory.

Despite my attempt to look disinterested, Ansley continued to talk.

"Whatever God has planned for you, will happen!" Ansley's raspy morning voice made the words sound so real and simple. I wished it were that easy for me, but it wasn't. I knew God had a plan for me and that's what made me sad. It didn't look like His plan was the same thing I wanted.

"What's the guy's name that she talked about— *Germ-o-my*—what's it again, Lena?"

"Jeremiah—it's a book in Bible," I answered.

Ansley pointed her finger at me. "Right! God's plans are good for you!"

Ansley was so pleased with her ability to remember last night's dinner devotion. I smiled at her. Her enthusiasm and excitement are always contagious.

"Trust God, Lena." She patted my shoulder and rested her head right above my elbow.

"I know the plans I have for you . . . Jeremiah 29:11. That's the verse." I mumbled and continued to talk. "But Ansley, did you understand what Mom and Dad were even saying? The whole story was little confusing, wasn't it?" I asked.

"What story?" Ansley suddenly had no idea what I was talking about.

I refreshed her memory. "Remember Dad told us about the Israelites and how God sent them to Babylon, the bad city, even though they didn't want to be there?"

"Ohhhh yeah, that's right." Ansley remembered.

"They were slaves there but that is where God needed them to be. But why?"

"I dunno," she replied quickly.

I could tell she was now the one losing interest but I kept talking. "Do you really think God would send us somewhere we didn't want to go or that was bad for us? I don't understand why He would do that."

"No, I don't get it either—why would God do that?" Ansley's words trailed off as she stared across the room and at the window above my bed. I wasn't sure if she was thinking about Babylon or the ice cream party we had scheduled for later on.

I just kept talking, "Well, no matter what happens with Mallory, I have my whole life planned out. I'm going to be a volleyball champion and an Olympic swimmer. I'll get married when I am twenty-four and have two children. I really want a boy and then a girl. I know I can't really plan that part but I'll talk to God about that when it's time. I know what makes me happy and what I am good at, so why would God not be happy with that? It would make no sense for Him to send me to a mean place or make me do something scary. I like it here in Texas with my family. Right?"

"I don't know, Lena. Just do what Germ-o-my says. Trust God." With those final words she bounced out of bed and went straight to her closet as if this conversation had fixed everything.

Maybe it had. I could feel my sadness starting to disappear and Ansley obviously had other things to worry about.

"Now, what am I going to wear today? It's Friday, we don't have school, and it's my birthday! Let's celebrate, Lena!" She swung open the two white closet doors and waited for me to join her.

Ansley was super excited to finally turn nine. She had been counting down since last year. Her eighth birthday announcement was, "I'm almost ten!" Even though she still had a year to go, I knew how excited she was to be one year closer.

I picked out her turquoise Converse because they are my favorite, a pair of long white socks, a pink tutu, and a gray sweatshirt with a big yellow smiley face on it.

I also put two little flowers in her hair with a side ponytail. She was definitely the cutest almost ten-year-old I'd ever seen.

Not long after I finished dressing Ansley, Ashton and Amber were awake and wanted in on my personal styling skills too.

Our morning quickly turned into a full-fledged family fashion show! When Mom heard the commotion she even invited us into her closet. Ashton found Mom's huge straw beach hat, her yellow spring scarf, and an old jean jacket. Amber and I wrapped Mom's skirts around us as dresses and picked out our favorite pairs of Mom's high heels. Ansley on the other hand loved her birthday outfit and decided to only play around with the pearl necklaces, bracelets, and earrings. Austin waddled between us until we finally found a little blue scarf for him too.

We click-clanked and paraded down the hall, through the living room, and in and out of the kitchen while Dad pretended to be our announcer, photographer, and audience.

The day was off to a better start than I'd imagined it would.

Eventually everyone was dressed in their final outfits and ready for Ansley's big adventurous day, which included a movie, ice cream, and friends!

The day was so fun and exciting that it wasn't until Mallory's voice came on the radio that I even remembered how badly I wanted her to call. I immediately wanted to turn the radio off but I couldn't because Ansley and her friends were bellowing. Every. Single. Word. I slouched down in my seat and prayed that no one saw how sad the entire scene was making me feel.

I didn't want to feel this way. It was silly and I felt so guilty about it. I knew I was being selfish and I wanted to hold back the tears but I just could not. I needed to get out of the car quickly.

When we pulled into the parking lot of the ice cream parlor I was the first one out.

"Be right back." I smiled in the direction of my mom and dad and escaped to the restroom as quickly as I could.

I stayed in the bathroom until my eyes were dry. I splashed them with water, squished them together tightly, and shook my head from side to side.

"God, I trust you," I whispered to myself and dashed through the large glass doors toward my family.

Ansley and one of her friends were spinning in circles, while Amber and the other ones were chasing each other around the table. Dad was just standing back and watching it all happen. They looked like a big herd of really cute chaos and seeing them forced a smile on my face.

I spotted Mom standing outside the ice cream shop. She was waving her phone in the air and motioning for Dad and me to join her.

"Hello . . ." She answered just as we reached her.

"Yes, this is she . . ." She glanced over at me and said, "Ok, hold on. I'll put it on speaker."

"Lena, this is for you," Mom said as she held the phone out.

I was so confused.

"It's on speaker," she added.

As I was grabbing it from her, I heard a very familiar voice. "Lena Daniels?" the voice said.

I hesitated.

"This is Mallory."

My words moved in slow motion from the back of my

brain to my mouth and they froze at my lips. My hands went numb while Mallory spoke.

"I just wanted to call all the girls that auditioned for the movie and thank them. I know it took a lot of courage to do that and I appreciate it so much! You are such a brave girl."

Still no words would come out of my mouth.

"As you can imagine," Mallory continued, "our team saw a lot of really great videos. It was almost impossible to choose just one girl but we had to. We prayed that God would show us which girl He wanted to have the part. So we want you to know that we take this very seriously. . . Lena? Are you there?"

I tried to force the word "yes" out of my mouth but I could not. Mom chimed in quickly, "Yes, she is." And now my sisters had come out to see what was going on.

I stood frozen. I had waited so long for this very phone call. My heart was beating super fast and I was concerned that my limbs would stop working at any moment.

Mallory continued, "I hope you aren't busy this summer because I want to know if you would consider joining us in Los Angeles, California to film the movie *Above the Waters* with me?"

I dropped to my knees in disbelief while my entire family let out a loud cheer! I covered my face with my hands and I could not tell if my voice was one of the ones screaming or sobbing.

"Lena? . . . Hello? . . . Is that a yes?"

Mallory was laughing and talking at the same time. "Are you guys ok?" she asked jokingly.

My dad's voice was the next one I heard clearly, "YES!" he shouted at the phone.

"Great! We are so excited to have Lena join us for this project! We truly believe she is amazing and just the girl God wants for the job. So, here's what will happen . . .

"The Fenways are the directors and producers of the movie. Either they or someone from their office will call you later on today to work out all the details. Everything will need to happen pretty quickly and they'll have all the information you need."

I started pulling myself off the ground as Mallory continued to talk. "In the meantime, do you have any questions for me?"

Mom and Dad were still grinning and Amber, Ashton, and Ansley wrapped themselves around my waist.

"No," I giggled. "Oh, wait! Yes! Will you be there the first day?"

"Absolutely! Looking forward to meeting you," Mallory responded.

Mom chimed in, "Well, Lena is super excited. We all are. She's sitting here speechless because she's laughing and crying so hard."

"Aw, I can't wait to meet you all!"

Mom continued, "I have another question. I know the movie is about a family learning to trust God. Right?"

"Yes, ma'am. It's about a family—a mom, dad, daughter, and grandmother. They are really close but the grandmother suddenly gets very ill. A number of significant and life-changing events happen, but in the end the family learns to trust God no matter the circumstance," Mallory answered.

"Oh, wow, that sounds like a fantastic story and message. Will Lena's role be considered a major part and how
long will she need to be there to film?"

"Lena, you do have a major part! You will be one of the
stars . . . exciting right?"

"YES!!" I was finally starting to calm down enough to
form words.

"Now as far as how long, that's a Mr. Fenway question.
This is my first movie so I don't understand it all yet either.
But the movie is going to be filmed in Los Angeles and I
think they film over an eight-week period. Now I know
that they will not film in the actual order of the movie.
So depending on when and how they schedule the scenes
that Lena is in will determine how long she needs to be
on set. They are finalizing those details today. Does that
make any sense?" Mallory sounded like she was trying to
convince herself too.

"Mmmm, yes, a little." Mom and Dad laughed and
Mallory joined them.

I didn't understand most of what Mallory had said
either. I was just trying to wrap my head around the fact
that Mallory Winston was on the phone with my family
like I'd pictured and hoped for so long. It was all actually
happening.

Mallory reassured us that Mr. Fenway would be calling
us very soon and he would have a lot more to tell us about
the entire process. She ended the conversation by asking
my dad to pray.

Dad prayed,

"Dear God, thank you so much for Mallory, the Fenway family, Lena, and all the other people that will work together on this project. I pray that as everyone starts to pull the pieces together, you would provide every detail from the right locations to the right cameras. We trust that you are orchestrating the details and we are grateful for the lives that will be impacted by this work. Bless this movie. Amen."

"Amen."

When we hung up, Mom led us all in one big shouting and screaming party. And Ansley's friends didn't hesitate to join in on the fun with us.

"So, Lena," Mom turned to look at me. "Are you ready to do this? Sounds like it could be a long summer in California. Are you ok with that?"

"Yes!" Ansley answered for me.

"Yes, ma'am!" I closed my eyes and thought, *thank you, God.*

We spent the rest of the day celebrating even more than we already had. I wanted to call Emma and Savannah but Mom asked me to wait until all the details were worked out.

That night, I lay in bed replaying the phone call over and over in my mind.

I sat up and scooted to the corner of my bed, right under my window.

I quietly slid my little black book from under my pillow.

I'd figured out just where to crawl in order to let the night's natural light from the window hit the pages on my journal.

Dear God,

I feel like I am starting all over! I wasn't sure if you heard my prayers when I asked that you let me get the call and the part! But now it really feels like you do hear me. Mom always says you work in silence and I wasn't sure what that meant. Now I guess I do, or at least I am trying to figure it out. You were so quiet and now look! You weren't saying anything but you were here. Thank you for answering my prayers and showing me that I really can trust you!! Wow!! Now God, I would have done things a little differently and a lot faster! But, oh well, I guess that's why I am NOT you! 'Cause you know the plans you have for me!

Yay! I am going to meet Mallory Winston! Thank you, God!!!!

Chapter 6

"Ouch," I moaned as I raised my head just enough to slide Ansley's yellow sandal from under my cheek. The room was dark and the only thing I could see was the reflection of sparkles.

Ansley had just gotten the sparkly sandals for her birthday and did not want to take them off. They were covered in rhinestones and green flowers. They looked like a baby tree decided to play dress up in a princess's closet! There was only one word that came to mind when I saw them—"Yuck!" But of course they were her favorite gift from her very special day.

I was actually surprised she didn't wear them to bed. But maybe she had. She probably wore them to bed and while she was sleeping her feet suddenly got a sense of style and kicked them off and across the room. Yes, that explained it.

But it didn't explain how I ended up on the floor with the sandals. Obviously there was much more going on here. Ansley and her rhinestones were not the only problem.

How exactly did I get down here? I wondered from my spot on the floor. I closed my eyes and tried to remember what happened.

I vaguely remembered a midnight bathroom break. But somehow I never managed to make it all the way back to my bed.

I pulled myself up off the floor, climbed back into bed, and squeezed my eyes shut. I could not see the clock, but I knew that it wasn't time to get up.

I rolled a little to left, then back to the right just a tiny bit, and tried to stop my mind from wandering.

I started chanting, "Sleep, sleep, sleep" in my head until I finally drifted off once again.

I woke up five hours later with Austin's little body sprawled across my bed. His wet tongue dangled from the corner of his mouth like that really big slip-and-slide Mom rented for Amber and Ashton's sixth birthday. Massive, wet, gross, and perfect.

He looked unconscious, so just to be sure he was fine I placed my index finger under his nose. First I felt heat escaping his nostrils and then in the next moment I started to hear a deep grumble coming from the bottom of his belly—I knew he was ok.

I stared at him for about four more seconds before gently shoving him off my bed and onto the pallet I'd made for him on the floor.

Seeing him lying there so comfortably made me chuckle. He didn't have a care in the world. "Oh, Austin, why were you in my bed? Are you nervous about meeting Mallory Winston too?" I laughed to myself. He just shifted his tongue to the other side and continued to snore.

I wasn't sure what time it was and if anyone else was awake so I slipped out of bed and tiptoed down the hall. The sound of my bedroom door creaking woke Austin and he followed behind me.

"Good morning, Sunshine!" Dad's words startled me.

I was still trying to adjust my eyes but suddenly I could hear a table full of chuckles and giggles.

Dad's smile was the first thing I saw at our kitchen table. That's because it was so big it covered the rest of his face.

Amber was using her pointer finger to clean the crumbs off her plate, Ashton was gnawing on a piece of bacon, while Mom was standing in front of the sink with bubbles up to her elbows.

I glanced around the kitchen and realized a lot had already happened this morning.

"Morning, guys." I plopped in the open seat next to Amber.

"Dad, have they called you yet?" I asked as Mom set a plate of eggs, two pancakes, and three slices of bacon in front of me. One whiff of bacon and I knew today was going to be good day.

"Yes, they did . . ." Dad paused, turned toward me, and continued. "So I spoke with the Fenways this morning, Gina and David."

"Yay!" I gasped. "What did they say?"

Dad stared at me intently. "They seem really nice. Mom and I talked to them for a while. They love God very much and this movie is an amazing opportunity for everyone involved. Unfortunately, they need you in California by Monday. Which means you need to leave tomorrow. And you'll need to be there until August ninth."

"Huh?" I almost laughed. "You're joking, right?"

Dad wasn't smiling. "No, Lena, I'm not. Mom and I have prayed and spoken about it and we think we have a plan to make it all work."

My mouth dropped open and suddenly my brain was full of so many thoughts! Monday was just a few days away. Two, to be exact. It was the end of the school year but I did still have a few days left and a few things I needed to do. I didn't want to interrupt my dad so I waited to tell him that that schedule would not work.

"You know it's in Los Angeles, right?" Dad was still talking to me.

"Yes." I kept my answer short because I wanted to hear everything else that Dad had to say.

"So your character's name is Jennifer and she's ten years old. Like Mallory told us, it's a pretty big part. Jennifer's family is struggling to believe that God is real until Jennifer becomes great friends with a woman named Nicole—that's Mallory."

My head was spinning. "Daddy, I can't be in California by Monday!" I blurted out.

"Yes, you can," Dad responded. "We asked if you could come just a few days later to give us some time, but unfortunately it's not possible. They need you there to start. That's why they are so excited they found you when they did. Without you, they wouldn't have been able to stay on schedule. So you and Mom will leave tomorrow. Your sisters and I will come by the end of the week, once school is finished. You know I can work from anywhere so that will not be a big deal."

He continued, "The Fenways are working on a house for us to stay in. They should have all the details by this evening, And we are going to book our flights in just a bit. We were just waiting for you to wake up!" Dad finished talking.

"See? God's working it all out!" Mom chimed in.

Every time I opened my mouth to speak, the words would just plop into the back of my throat and stay there. I kept my eyes glued on my dad. I could not believe the words that were coming out of his mouth.

Mom used my silence as an opportunity to continue with more of the details. "They sent the script over, so after breakfast you can take a look at it. I printed it already and Lena, you have lots of lines! It looks like you are in almost every scene!"

I sat staring at them. I was in shock and did not how to respond.

The people talking looked like my mom and dad but my parents would never be this calm about moving our entire family to California in a week. They were talking as if this was all very normal. But none of it was normal.

This was the complete opposite of normal. It felt strange and I wanted to let them know what I thought.

"This is . . . mmmm . . . well, a little crazy, right?" The words flew out of my mouth as if I had no control over them. As soon as I said them, I knew I shouldn't have.

I could tell from Dad's face that he was not happy with what I had said.

"Hold on now, Lena." Dad's voice was louder than normal.

"Sorry Daddy. But I can't leave tomorrow. It's not possible. I still have school and my friends. And what about my plans for the summer? Emma just invited Savannah and me to go to Mexico with her!"

Dad stopped me from speaking any further. "Lena, I'm

sorry about that. But remember you asked for this. You said yes to this opportunity yesterday and now your mother and I are trying to figure out how to make it all work with the family. And there are lots of people counting on you and your commitment to the movie. So if you seriously don't think you want to do it, let us know right now."

I interrupted my dad. "Daddy, that's not what I mean. I just don't see how I can pack today, board an airplane tomorrow with a movie script in one hand and my entire life in the other, and head off to an unknown place with unknown . . ."

Dad interrupted me this time. "I get that it is a lot to take in, Lena. But if you really don't think you can do this then tell us now before everyone involved continues making plans. Not just us but the Fenways too."

Suddenly ten eyeballs were all staring in my direction. My sisters sat around the table listening, and no one was smiling anymore.

Mom sat down next to me.

I could not tell if she and Dad were angry, frustrated, disappointed, or a combination of all three but I knew this was serious and I knew I needed to think carefully.

I wanted this opportunity. I had cried for it. I had prayed for it. I just had no idea about everything it would involve. I had no idea it would mean leaving so soon. I would not even have a chance to say goodbye to my friends. I would miss my school awards banquet on Tuesday, my class party on Wednesday, and my entire summer! And what about Austin, what was the plan for him?

Is this really what I want now? I never actually wanted

to be an actress, I just wanted to meet Mallory Winston. What would she think of me if I changed my mind? I really needed to think about this. I wished I could talk to Emma and Savannah. They would know what I should do.

My eyes began to water and I knew that I was going to burst into tears. I had cried a lot lately and once the tears started it was hard to stop them.

"Lena," Mom started. "I want you to know that it really is ok if you don't want to do this. Being in a movie requires a lot of work and a lot change that you probably have not thought about. But I also want you to think about the idea that maybe this opportunity is from God. Sometimes God asks us to do things that we don't really want to do. Sometimes it's scary and uncomfortable but He wants us to trust Him."

Mom placed her hand on top of mine and spoke softly.

"Lena, I want you to remember that you prayed about this. Do you think that maybe this is something that God is asking you to do? Now that things look more challenging, can you still trust Him?"

"Yes, but why would God care if I do this or not? I do trust Him . . ." I paused. My words were full of emotions. "Mmm, well, I *try* to trust him. But does He really care if I am in a movie?"

"God cares about you and every detail of your life, Lena. Everything."

Dad spoke, "And sometimes He asks us to do things that we don't understand because we can't see the whole picture. But God does. Remember what God does for you is not just for you. He wants to use you to show others His love. He even wants to grow you and teach you things so that He can use you even more."

I sunk back in my seat and pushed my plate forward. My eggs were cold and my bacon didn't even look good anymore.

I knew my mom and dad were right. I remembered crying and praying that if this was God's plan I would get this opportunity. But that was when it seemed fun. Now suddenly it all just seemed really, really hard.

In my heart I understood what God was asking me to do, yet somehow that didn't make me feel any better about the changes to my plans. And it definitely didn't make it less hard.

I felt my heartbeat begin to slow down and although I still had lots of questions, I managed to smile.

"Ok." I forced the word out of my mouth.

Ansley had been sitting on the edge of her seat waiting. Shifting her eyes back and forth from Dad to me to Mom and back to me. As soon as she heard the word, "Ok," from me, she said, "So then yes, Lena? 'Cause I'm going to need to start packing! And so do you!"

We all chuckled and I reached over and gave Ansley a squeeze.

Dad looked at me said, "Lena, remember what Jeremiah 29:11 says, 'For I know the plans I have for you, declares the Lord, plans for welfare and not for evil, to give you a future and a hope.' Sweetie, trust that God has this all worked out."

My mind was racing with so many thoughts. I needed to pack. I needed to talk to Emma and Savannah and I needed to find a way to make everything make sense.

I excused myself from the table and headed to my room.

I laid across my bed with Austin. I needed to talk to someone. And I was sure there was only one person who would understand.

Hello, God,

Ok. So I am not sure what you are doing or if you are even doing anything. Are you? I wish there was a way to really talk to you. I mean, I know I can talk to you but I wish you would talk back. For a while it seemed like you didn't want me to get this part and I prayed and prayed that you did. Now all of sudden it seems like you do. So why me? I am so confused. Mom and Dad keep saying you care about my life and to trust you and that you have a plan. But if I don't know your plan, then how do I know if I am doing the right thing? This is so hard! I don't want to mess up.

Ok, I'll go. Just please don't let me mess up.

Chapter 7

The next morning, I woke up at sunrise. The funny thing is I was in my closet on the floor, balled up in a tangle of blankets and last week's uniform shirts, socks, and skirts.

"So weird," I whispered quietly.

It was Sunday. I was all set to leave in just a few hours. My life felt like complete chaos and so did the inside of my stomach.

The last fourteen hours had been a whirlwind. Plane tickets were purchased, emails to my teachers and friends were sent, our new summer home was ready, and everything I needed for the summer was stuffed into my large lime green suitcase, my turquoise duffle bag, and my green and turquoise polka-dot backpack.

The room was still mostly dark and the house was silent.

Well, silent with a few alternating moments of deep breaths, snorts, and whimpers. So, ok, I guess it was not really silent at all. But when no one is talking, I find comfort in these sounds—the sounds of my family. I may be the only one awake, but at least I wasn't alone. From my open bedroom door I could see Ashton and Amber across the hall, sleeping under their pink and turquoise flowered comforter and I knew Mom and Dad were just a few steps away.

I just lay there listening for a moment.

"Lena!" Mom's whisper interrupted my thoughts. I hadn't even heard her coming.

"Yes?" I said while quietly scooting forward through my closet doors.

Mom looked surprised to see me crawling on the floor. "What are you doing?"

I shrugged. I didn't have an answer for her because I had no idea how I ended up there. Must have been another midnight bathroom run gone wrong.

"Alrightyyyy then," she said and quickly moved on as if my sleeping on my closet floor was completely normal. "Emma and Savannah are coming over! I just hung up with them."

I leaped in the air and landed one foot at a time, trying not to make a lot of noise as my bare feet thumped against the floor.

"Yay! Thank you, Mommy!!" I squealed in a whisper, if that's possible.

"Welcome, sweetie. It's still early but they will be over in about an hour. They can only stay for a little bit, but at least you will get to see them both before our flight." Mom finished speaking but her words lingered and so did her smile.

"What time is it anyway?" I asked.

"It's 7:40."

"Ok." I headed directly down the hall for the shower. Knowing that Emma and Savannah were coming gave me the energy I needed to get the day started.

By nine o'clock Emma and Savannah were at the door and I was one happy girl.

Needless to say we skipped church because of all the chaos. Dad invited Emma and Savannah to stay for a big breakfast and an at-home church time.

He put us girls in charge of worship. We chose our favorite Mallory Winston songs and Amber and Ashton created dance and hand motions to match. We giggled way more than we sang and when it was time for Dad to talk he could barely get us to calm down.

He gathered us all around the kitchen table and just repeated, "Girls, girls, girls . . ." until finally the room was quiet and all eyes were focused on him.

"Ok . . . now that I have everyone's attention, I just want to take few minutes to talk before Lena heads off for her great big awesome adventure this summer."

Savannah and Emma both pretended to sob momentarily. Dad smiled and continued, "Last night I was praying about this summer and what it would mean for our family. Lena, would you believe that Mom and I are a little scared?"

Dad's confession surprised me. I had had no idea but he had my full attention. Knowing my parents felt like I did somehow made me feel better.

"It can be scary taking such a big jump and doing something so different than what we normally do. But for some reason I kept thinking about Peter."

"Peter that walked on water, Daddy?" Amber asked.

"Yup, Amber. That's him. He walked on water. Actually Peter knew a lot about water because he was a fisherman, so he knew how crazy it was to ask God to help him walk on water. He knew that people could not really walk on water. The people around him probably thought he was ridiculous for even asking. And that's the thing—Peter had crazy faith in God. Don't you think?"

It felt like Dad was looking at each of us in the eye at the same time. We all nodded and Dad kept right on talking.

"Peter did not let what people thought stop him. He didn't even let what he already knew about water stop him from trusting God for something so big! He still asked God for something crazy! Peter believed and trusted God to do impossible things.

"So Lena, Emma, Savannah, Amber, Ashton, and Amber, I pray that no matter where you are or what is going on around you, you will always be crazy for God."

His words landed on my ears but like silly putty, some stuck there while the rest slowly slid down and settled into the center of my heart. Something told me I would need to keep them there forever.

I smiled and said, "I'll always be crazy, Dad."

Ashton chimed in, "Mmm-hmmm!"

We all chuckled. I felt better than I had in hours. I still wasn't sure I understood it all but spending so much time with my family and friends made everything feel right. I may not have known what I was doing but I knew I wasn't making a mistake.

Savannah and Emma left at eleven and by 11:20 Dad was loading the van with a summer's worth of Mom's and my belongings.

It was quiet for most of the ride to the airport until Ansley blurted out, "Lena, you are going to meet Mallory Winston soon!"

"AHHHHHHHHHHHHH!" I screamed.

Between all the tears, gummy teeth, prayers, luggage, and goodbyes I had somehow lost track of the fact that meeting her was really happening.

"I wonder what she's like."

It did not sound like Ansley wanted an answer but Ashton gave her one anyway, "Awesome."

Ironically, Ashton's one word reply summed up everything I was feeling. Awesome. It felt awesome to know that God had answered my prayers. It felt awesome to know that my friends and family were just as excited as I was. And it felt awesome to know that I was just hours away from meeting Mallory.

As soon as Mom and I boarded the plane, I opened my book bag and pulled out my little black book. I turned to the next empty page and wrote the word: AWESOME in big box letters across the entire page.

After taking a little time to carefully color in each and every letter I glided my hand to the next empty page and wrote:

Dear God,

This is awesome. Thank you.

Chapter 8

"Flight attendants, please prepare for landing."

Mom slept the entire flight and I must have joined her. The loud yet muffled voice coming from the little speakers in the ceiling made me jump. Mom popped up just as the flight attendant was motioning for her to pull her seat forward.

I knew that Mom had slept well because when she sat up she was smacking her lips together and looking around trying to figure out where she was.

She turned towards me, frowned a little, and gasped.

"Mom, what is it?" I was panicked.

She had a look of terror in her eyes. I had no idea what it could be until she said, "Lena, your hair!"

Now I was really worried. "What? What is it? What is wrong with my hair?"

I reached my hand to the top of my head and touched it. One big sticky glob of hair right in the front.

My mom sat there staring.

"Mom, help me! What is it?"

"Gum," she replied.

My hair was covered in sticky, grapy, purple gum. GUM . . . I tried to tug it out but then I realized pulling would just make it worse.

Mom was still not helping and I was starting to feel a little annoyed. I am not sure if she was half asleep or just enjoyed watching me pull my hair out strand by strand like some sort a fanatic. Either way I needed her to do something and she wasn't.

"Welcome to California," the pilot announced just as we felt the wheels vibrating across the ground.

This was a disaster. We had arrived, my mom was in a total traveler's trance, and my perfectly cute, freshly straightened hair had become a messy, gooey, gum-hawk.

Once we finally made our way off the plane and into the airport terminal, we headed straight for a restroom.

Mom was finally awake, alert, and moving fast.

As soon as we burst through the doors, she pulled out her little clear plastic fix-it pouch. She sat it on one of the sinks and started digging—pulling out thread, insect repellant, and hair spray. I'm not sure what she was looking for and I didn't have time to find out. I stood at the sink next to her, turned on the faucet, bent down, and pushed as much of the top of my head directly under the tiny spout as I could. Water splashed everywhere, my hair was ruined, and I still felt globs of gum.

Mom muttered, "Oh, goodness." Followed by, "Ahhh, here they are! Clippers!"

"You mean nail clippers?" I shouted! "No way, Mom!"

Meanwhile I could hear movement coming from the back of the restroom and a few seconds later there was a flush from one of the stalls.

I gasped and mumbled under my breath, "Uh oh, Mom . . . we are not alone."

"Yeah, it's ok. Let's just focus on getting this hair taken care of," she replied.

My initial thought was to stand up straight and pretend nothing unusual was happening with my hair, my mother, or me. Something inside of me would not let me. I agreed with Mom, we needed to just stay focused on my clump of hair. I was determined to somehow remove this two-hour-old gum. So, I just kept right on drowning my head in the sink.

I heard a door swing open, and knew it was just a matter of seconds before total embarrassment set in. I braced myself as I tilted my head from under the running water just enough to get a peek at who was coming toward me.

"Uh-oh," Mom mumbled under her breath. "Lena, sweetie," I felt Mom tugging at my arm.

Out of the corner of my eye I could see two purple cowboy boots swiftly moving, one in front of the other. A long white skirt flowed in line with the shifting of each pointy-toed boot. Without even seeing a face, I knew who it was.

"Get up," Mom tried to urge.

I immediately raised my head from under the running water, my wet gummy hair flung forward and I watched as splatters of water sailed across the restroom and land on the blue jean shirt of Mallory Winston.

"Oh no!!" Mom gasped.

Mallory stopped walking, blinked a few times really fast and backed away.

"We are so sorry." Mom moved frantically towards the towel dispenser pulling and pulling.

With water dripping from the top of my head down my shoulders, I stood tall and announced, "Uhhhhhhh. Hi, I'm Lena."

Mallory opened her eyes wide.

"Lena Daniels," I continued.

Mom stepped forward and held out her handful of little white squares.

Mallory politely took the paper towels from my mother and inched a little closer towards me. She stooped down until we were the same height and spoke with so much joy in her voice, "Hi, Lena. It's me, Mallory!"

"Oh, we know," Mom said nervously. "So nice to meet you."

"I'm so sorry," I uttered.

"Oh no, don't worry." Mallory waved her hand in the air and tried to act as normal as possible. "Hmm, it's just a little water on me. But what do we have going on here?"

"Gum," Mom answered and pointed to the top of my head.

Mallory dropped her big brown leather bag on the floor and buried her head between the two thick straps.

"I think I have just what you need. You probably should get used to wearing these anyway, you know, so people won't keep stopping you for pictures. I mean, you are going to be famous now!" She chuckled while shuffling things around until she found what she was looking for.

Finally, she pulled out the cutest white baseball cap I had ever seen. It had a big turquoise "2" on the front and a thin yellow line tracing the brim.

She plopped it right on top my wet hair and smiled. "Ok, ladies, shall we go? I think we have a car waiting for the three of us!"

"Oh, perfect!" Mom cheered as she helped me gather

our things. "Mallory," she started, "you are a life saver! I didn't know what we were going to do. Now I'm sure I can get it out once we get settled." Mom thought for a moment and said, "I didn't realize we were riding together."

Mallory explained that she was just flying in from a concert in Florida. The production team had scheduled us to be picked up from the airport together to make things easier.

I walked just a little behind Mallory and Mom and watched. They talked to each other as if they had known each other for years. Mom kept glancing in my direction and inviting me into their conversation with her smile. I was too nervous to speak. Mallory was taller than I thought she'd be and she smelled like sugar-covered strawberries. Her boots were loud and her skirt created a welcome breeze for me when she walked.

Mom had lots of questions about the movie and what exactly was going on, but Mallory had very few answers. They both seemed to enjoy talking it all through anyway.

I had made so many mistakes already with my gummy teeth and gummy hair. I didn't want to do or say anything else to embarrass myself. I just soaked up Mallory's words and tried to remember every detail of our first few moments. I knew Emma and Savannah would want to hear all about it.

While waiting for our bags Mallory stood next to me and directed her words right to me.

"I'm pretty nervous about our first day. Are you, Lena?"

"Uhhh, yeah, a little." I exhaled, giggled, and answered.

"A little?" Mom teased as she pulled me close and gave me a big squeeze.

Mallory laughed and so did I. "Ok, yeah, a lot!"

"I've known the Fenway family for a long time and they are so nice. They love God so much and are the best. You'll love them. Oh here's my bag!"

Mallory raced towards the slow moving carousal and reached for her all black bag with the dangling purple cowboy boot keychain.

"I'll head out and find our ride!"

Mom and I both said ok and watched as she whisked her bag away and exited through the glass doors.

"Lena," Mom said, "she's great!"

"Yup." She was definitely that.

Mom was still talking but I couldn't really move my mouth to respond. This entire experience was starting to feel more and more like a dream. I didn't know whether to scream with excitement or run far away to stop myself from waking up.

Mom and I finally got our luggage. Mallory was waiting for us directly outside the door. She was standing in front of a big black SUV with dark tinted windows waving her hand to make sure we saw her.

"Over here!" she shouted.

Mom and I rolled our bags over to the curb. We were welcomed to California by the driver before hopping in.

Mom and Mallory continued to talk while I tried to pretend I wasn't still in shock.

We all agreed to stop for dinner before we headed to our new home.

Dinner was fun and I could feel myself getting more and more comfortable around Mallory. She was so much more than I even imagined and I was excited to get to know her more. By the time we arrived at the house, I was exhausted and so was Mom.

Except for some reason I couldn't sleep. So after I laid in my new bed a while, I pulled out my journal.

Hello, Stars,

I thought about Peter a lot today. I guess when I asked God to give me this opportunity, it was kinda like asking Him to help me walk on water! A lot of people thought I was crazy . . . even I did. Now that I am here it feels like I am in the middle of a big ocean and I better keep looking to Him for help.

God, please help me not to sink.

Amen.

Chapter 9

"Ouch!"

My eyes sprang open as my cheek slammed into the floor.

I stared up at my empty bed from the middle of my new bedroom floor. I closed my eyes and tried to recall how I'd gotten there. I really needed to figure out why I was not able to wake up in the same place I went to bed.

Moments before I landed on the floor I was standing on the right side of a volleyball net in my school's gym. Emma and Savannah were on my team and Ms. Blount was the coach. It was my turn to serve. My arms were shorter than everyone else's and I could hear the opposing team screaming for me to hurry. I was so afraid to try but jumped in the air anyway, flung my arm back, and landed on the floor . . .

Was I dreaming? I thought as I looked around in the dark. There was no trace of a volleyball, a net, or even a gym floor. I was just lying on the beige carpet in between two empty beds.

A few seconds later I heard a voice in the dark, "Lena, are you ok?"

I tried to lift my head but it felt too heavy.

"Did you just fall out of the bed?" the voice spoke again. "Come on, get up and get back in bed."

I felt two strong arms pulling me off the floor and guiding me toward my bed.

"Mommy?"

"Yes, Lena. It's me. Did you have a bad dream?"

"No, well, I don't know, this just keeps happening—almost every night."

Mom pulled my blanket up over my tummy and whispered, "God, will you help Lena to relax? I pray that you comfort her and bring peace to her mind so that she can rest well. Amen." Mom kissed me on my forehead and added, "You have to stop worrying about things so much and learn to trust God. When you are stressed, you don't sleep well and it can make you cranky! Now take a few deep breaths and try to go back to sleep."

As soon as I heard Mom exit the room, my eyes popped open wider. I was back in bed and suddenly wide awake.

It was too quiet to sleep. There were no covers rustling from Ansley's side of the room and I couldn't hear Ashton and Amber whimpering and snorting from across the hall.

The new house was nice but it was not home. It smelled like a mix of paint and cardboard boxes. Mom said we just needed to add a couple of things to make it feel homey. She thought a few bathroom floor mats, shower curtains, and a bunch of random new-home-must-have items will do the trick. I thought it just needed my dad, sisters, and Austin. It had only been one day without them but it felt like forever!

I felt lonely and I was afraid. I kept trying to imagine what my first day on set would be like. I wondered how Mr. Fenway would treat me. Or if once he met me he would change his mind about me being in the movie.

I slowly sat up and dangled my feet off the edge of the bed. I stared through the open bedroom door and tried to remember which way lead to my mom's room. My room felt too lonely to stay. I wandered down the hall and stood there for a few seconds before deciding it was to the right. I tiptoed in and with both of my hands stretched out, I guided myself right into the bed next to Mom.

Mom didn't utter a word until I was completely snuggled under her blankets and settled into the crease of her elbow.

"Can't sleep, huh? Are you ok?"

I nodded but we both knew I didn't mean it.

"Are you excited for your first day on set?" Thankfully Mom continued to probe because all I needed was one more question.

"I am. I think. Well . . ." I rolled over so that I could see her. Her eyes were still shut but I knew she was listening.

"I'm really scared. I don't want to mess up."

"Oh, Lena, you don't need to be scared," Mom assured me as she opened her eyes to look at me now.

"But what if I can't memorize my lines? Or say them right? I mean, it's not like I am an actress. I have no idea what I am doing. What if they are mean?"

Mom interrupted my outburst, "Lena, do you think you got a major part in a major movie because of something you did?"

Her question made me pause. I wasn't sure what she meant and I was hoping she would keep talking, but she didn't. She just stared at me for a moment. The room was dark but the whiteness of her eyes was bright and reminded me of two big headlights on a dark road. I sat up and stared back at her.

"Well?" she said. She wanted an answer.

"Well, I guess." I was sure this wasn't the answer she wanted but I wasn't sure what else to say. I let my words linger and hoped that my silence would urge her to explain.

"Oh, really."

Oh, really? Was that really all she was going to say?

"I mean, I auditioned for it," I continued.

"Lena, hundreds of girls sent their videos in to Mallory. Do you really think you got the part just because of your video?"

"Well, I prayed for it. Is that what you mean?"

"We pray for lots of things. Praying doesn't always mean that God gives you exactly what you want. Praying is a way that you put God in charge of giving you what He wants for you. It's also a way to let Him know that you trust Him."

Mom continued to talk, "I think you are worried so much because you are forgetting something really important. You are forgetting that He is in charge! Lena, you didn't get a part in a movie because you auditioned and you didn't get it because you have worked hard as an actress. You even just said that you aren't an actress. You are here in California because this is where God wants you. He gave you this opportunity. The only thing you did was say yes to it!"

Mom seemed wide awake. She spoke with confidence and I believed every word she was saying.

"You don't have to worry about not being the right one for it. He has already said you are. So now you just have to be His daughter. He will take care of all the other pieces. No need to stress about how you will do, remember God's got it. You just do your best and He will make you what He needs you to be!"

"Mommy, I am so confused. You and Daddy keep telling me to have faith, to trust God, and that He has plans for me. But somehow this is all still very hard. I think I just don't get it. I really wanted to meet Mallory but my life was so much easier before all of this started."

I wasn't crying but my voice was a bit screechy. I had so many questions but my words were all jumbled in my foggy, sleepless brain. I flopped back onto her pillows and let out a deep rumbly breath.

"I know, Lena. It's all a part of growing up and growing in your relationship with God. Trusting Him is not easy. Remember Peter? Sometimes trusting God means you have to do something crazy! But you have to do it, no matter how crazy it is. Sometimes I don't get it all either. I just talk to God and let Him know how I'm feeling. You can do that too. He will keep teaching you and showing you what He wants you to do and how He wants you to do it. I believe this movie is just God's way of teaching you that He is in charge and that you can trust Him. He's got big plans for you. Way bigger than anything you can do by yourself. So stop stressing and just rest, Lena. Now, you need to get some sleep and so do I. Morning will be here before we know it."

I lay there quietly next to Mom. I tossed to the right, she rolled to the left. I kicked one leg from underneath her blankets and she pulled the comforter up close under her chin. Mom exhaled and smacked her lips together, I inhaled and rubbed my eyes. We each twitched, squirmed, and struggled to find sleep again.

Finally it became clear that neither of us would get any rest like this. Even though my brain was still full of thoughts, the house felt lonely and my stomach now felt empty. I headed back to my own bed feeling grateful for our talk. I needed to process all Mom had to say. I picked up my little black book.

Dear God,

Lately it always feels like Mom and even Dad are talking in code. I wish they would just tell me exactly what to do to and make all these confusing words go away. I bet Mallory is not up stressing about being in a movie. She's probably resting. Well, I want to rest too! But how can I, when there is so much new stuff happening and so much pressure to do it right? Resting should be easy but this is hard! Does Mom mean don't work hard? That can't be. She always tells me to work hard and to do my best. Can you please tell me how I am supposed to trust you, do something crazy, and relax all at the same time? And why do I need to learn all this now? I just want to become besties with Mallory! I really want to relax right now.

Chapter 10

The next sound I heard was my little clock buzzing next to my bed letting me know it was time to get up.

"Mom! It's time to get up!" I called from my bedroom.

"Ok, I'm up. I'm up." she said twice—once to convince me and I think the other was to convince herself.

It was 7:00 and I was scheduled to arrive on set at 8:00 am sharp.

"Mom, please hurry! We are going to be late!" I hurried out of bed and headed across the hall to my bathroom to brush my teeth.

Mom lay still for a few more seconds before I finally heard her start to move around.

While swooshing the minty blue mouthwash around in my mouth for a few more seconds, I pictured Ansley, Ashton, and Amber running around getting ready for school. I wondered what they had eaten for breakfast and if they had a chance to play with Austin first. Poor Austin, he must have been so sad and worried when he didn't see me heading out with the others this morning.

"Lena!" Mom was standing at my door. To my surprise she was smiling. "It's Daddy, he wants to FaceTime!"

My ears perked up and I felt a wave of energy swarm its way into each of my tired limbs. I emptied my mouth while grabbing the phone right out of Mom's hand.

"Good morning, sleepy head!" Dad said while smiling from ear to ear.

"Hi, Daddy!" I squealed.

Dad continued, "So I heard you had quite an introduction yesterday and that your hair had a traumatic experience while flying!"

"Oh, Daddy," I chuckled. "It was terrible!" I started to laugh uncontrollably while attempting to fill him in on every single detail. He laughed right along with me.

Dad always had a way of making me laugh at myself. None of it seemed so bad after hearing him joke about it.

Dad gathered himself and said, "Ok, let me pray over you and Mom before you go. Today is going to be great. Remember who has you there!"

Then he prayed,

"Dear God, I thank you for Lena. You have created her strong and beautiful on the outside and on the inside. I pray that when people meet and see her, they see you first. Lord, continue to build your character in her. As Galatians 5 says, I pray that she be full of love, joy, peace, patience, kindness, goodness, faithfulness, gentleness, and self-control. In Jesus' name . . ."

"Amen!" I chimed in.

Seeing Dad's face and praying with him was exactly what Mom and I needed to get us ready for the day. Within a few moments we were both fully dressed and ready to go.

Mom was told there would be a car outside of our house waiting. We ran toward the front door excited to begin this new adventure.

"Oh," Mom said as she opened the front door and

spotted a bright yellow spaceship-looking vehicle that was sitting right outside our new home. My mom looked at me and I knew exactly what she was thinking. It was hideous.

It looked as if the windows and lights had been put on backwards. The lights were little squares while the windows reminded me of the large bubbles I once made during a science experiment. The front of the car looked like a box and the back looked smashed.

Whether we liked it or not, we were going to have to drive that thing around all summer long. Mom tried to pretend it wasn't that bad and told me to be grateful that we even had a car. I tried my best not to, but it was pretty hard not to laugh at that thought. I was certain that people driving by us would be laughing too.

We hopped in, buckled up, and just when I thought we were ready to pull off, Mom opened her navy blue plastic folder with all the information we needed. She used her pointer finger to skim through a lot of small printed words.

She began rambling, "Ok, so today we need to go right to the studio. It should only take us seven minutes to get there . . . what time is it? It's 7:49. Ok, great, you will be right on time. Uhhhh, you will not go here every day because they will film at different locations . . . sometimes a car will pick you up . . . wardrobe . . . scene one . . ."

Her voice trailed off and she started to sound like she was chewing six gumballs under water. I no longer had any idea what she was talking about.

"Mom, I can't understand you," I tried to say calmly even though I could feel myself getting a little frustrated.

I took a deep breath and waited patiently for her to finish.

She mumbled for a few more seconds and my ears perked up when I heard her says words like hair, makeup, and breakfast.

Once she was finished, she tossed the folder into my lap.

I smiled and opened the folder myself. I read each line carefully as Mom typed an address in her phone's GPS, adjusted her mirrors, and looked out her side window.

Just before she pushed the gas pedal she blurted, "Blast off!!"

We basically giggled all the way to the studio. I needed to laugh to keep my brain from thinking too much. I had no idea what to expect and feelings of panic and pure terror were trying to take over my brain. No matter how hard I tried to imagine everything ahead I just could not.

We pulled into the dark, winding three-floor parking garage and found an empty spot right near some glass doors.

"Thank you, Lord," Mom said with a sigh of relief. She parked the car and hopped right out. I didn't move.

Our eyes met through the car window and she said, "Well, what are you waiting for? Come on!"

"Here we go." I hesitated before using my black and white high top Converse to push open the door.

Mom grabbed my hand and we headed toward the entrance. We were about ten footsteps away when the glass doors flung open and a girl dressed all in black came racing toward us.

"Lena?" she asked.

I felt my mom squeeze my hand as I nodded.

The girl was moving fast. She flung her arms around me and squealed.

"So fun to finally meet you! I'm Kay B and I'm a production assistant. Well, I'm actually just an intern. I'm basically here to make sure you get where you need to be when you need to be there and help you with anything else you need!"

She barely took a breath so Mom and I just stood still and listened.

"Come on, let's get you in here before you are late!"

We followed her through the doors, down a tiny hallway, and into a large classroom. It was nothing like I expected. "What kind of movie set is this?" I said to myself. I looked at Mom and she gave me her "It's ok, Lena" smile.

People were sitting at a really big white U-shaped table with plates of food and papers spread out in front of them.

As we stepped through the door Kay B announced, "Hey everyone, here is Lena!"

There was an immediate uproar and everyone was smiling, cheering, and saying things to me. Things like: "I'm Michael," "Sit here," and "Awww, you are so adorable."

If I could have disappeared at that very moment I would have.

Despite what I was feeling, I mimicked Mom's expression and plastered the biggest smile possible on my face while the crowd continued to examine me.

I heard a voice from behind me. I turned around and was greeted by a massive outstretched hand and a friendly smile. "Hi, Lena. I'm David Fenway. We are so glad you are here."

I reluctantly held out my sweaty palm and prayed he didn't notice how nervous I was.

"How's it going so far? Everything ok with the house and the car and your flights?"

A picture of the yellow spaceship flashed across my mind and I smiled. "Yes, sir. Everything is great."

"So glad to hear it. Today should be fun. After the meeting, I want you and Mallory to stick around. We'll go over your first scene!" He motioned to the right and told me to grab something to eat before we got started.

I followed his gesture and could not believe my eyes. There was a huge table covered with brown-sugar-coated blueberry muffins, bowls of fluffy, pink yogurt, gorgeous mounds of assorted fruit, and rows of sprinkle-covered donuts—which of course made me feel right at home.

I dashed right over, grabbed a few of my favorite things, and found the empty seat right next to Mallory. She wrapped one arm around my shoulders as I sat down and gave me a little squeeze.

"So far so good," I thought. I pulled out the navy folder Mom had given me in the car, my pink and white striped notepad, and my "I Love Paris" pen.

I was ready for whatever was next even if it meant non-stop talking for an hour!

Mr. Fenway led the discussion on dates, deadlines, lights, props, and a lot of other things. He passed out huge white binders which contained the script, schedule, and important phone numbers. I was trying really hard to keep up but mostly I had no idea what they were talking about.

He discussed the filming process and confirmed

everything that Mallory had already told me and Mom. The movie would film over several weeks in different locations within the surrounding cities. He explained the filming process just like Mallory had, and I am not sure that Mom or I understood it any better. He wanted us to know that it may seem weird but we would film the end of the movie first because that location was already available. We would then work our way backwards and film different scenes—because they "film based on location instead of timeline."

When I heard this I drew a huge question mark across the first page of my binder. Mallory chuckled.

As the room emptied out I sat alone at the big white table nervously waiting for my next directions. Mom was in the hall talking and I was pretending to look over the script. After a few minute Mallory came back and joined me.

"Phew," she said as she took a seat. "You ok, Lena?" Mallory pulled out her phone and starting to flip through her messages.

I tried really hard to think of something to say but all that came out was, "Yup."

After a few seconds of awkward silence Mr. Fenway hurried over to join us.

I'm not sure how much coffee he had during the meeting but his voice was loud and full of energy.

"Lena Daniels and Mallory Winston!" He was standing over the top of us. His smile was just as loud as his words. "Are you both ready to have some fun? We're making a movie!"

Mallory jumped to her feet. "Yes, sir, we are!"

I hopped up and tried to match their excitement. "I'm ready too!"

The words sat in the air for a few seconds and I felt silly.

Mr. Fenway rubbed his hands together, bit his bottom lip, and scanned the big empty room. "Hmmm," he started to speak. "Where should we start . . ."

Both Mallory and I watched and listened without interrupting his thoughts.

"Let's just stay here and read over your first scene together. Then I'll take you over to the set and give you a little tour. How's that sound?"

"Perfect."

"Yup, perfect," I agreed.

"Ok. We will start from page 196, all the way toward the back of your notebook. When you come tomorrow you won't need to bring the book. Kay B will have sides for you."

"Sides?" Mallory questioned.

"Oh, yes, you will get those daily. Just a small piece of paper with all the information that you need for the day, like times, scenes, and lines. Lena, Kay B will probably email them to your Mom the night before and then just give you a copy when you get here as well."

I smiled. Something about Mr. Fenway made me feel comfortable and calm. He didn't look like I'd imagined him. He was wearing a pair of jeans and a plain yellow T-shirt. His outfit reminded me of my dad. His voice was soothing and Mallory and I both followed every direction he gave. By the time we finished practicing our lines I felt better prepared and more excited.

When I told Mom all about it later that night, she simply looked at me and said, "See—just relax!"

I wasn't completely convinced, but I was starting to feel more relaxed.

Hello, Stars,

Today was so much better than I imagined! Mr. Fenway is super nice and so was everyone else. Best of all, I got to spend a lot of time with Mallory. I am so happy right now and super excited for tomorrow.

   Dear God,

   Can you please keep showing me how to relax and trust you? It feels so much better when I do!

   God, thank you for a good day.

Chapter 11

"Good morning, everyone!"

Mr. Fenway started every day the exact same way. He stood in the middle of the floor wearing a pair of bulky black headphones around his neck, holding a handful of papers. He always looked busy but he never seemed to be in a rush. Somehow he managed to focus his eyes and attention on everyone in the room at the same time.

He began by reminding everyone what scene we were working on. Next he would point out a few notes regarding the schedule right before he asked us all to join hands for prayer. I loved starting each day this way because it reminded me of home. I knew people loved God but I never thought there were other people who did the same things my family did.

"Thank you, everyone, for a phenomenal week," Mr. Fenway began. "I could not have asked for a better group of people to work with on this film. When Gina and I produced our first film seven years ago, we didn't have a lot of resources or people that wanted to help us. Now, when I look around at all of you, I am so grateful. We had no idea that God would do so many amazing things with our little dream of making movies that entire families could enjoy."

Mr. Fenway paused and closed his eyes.

I sat at a table between my mother and Kay B and

soaked in every detail Mr. Fenway shared. He seemed so relaxed and smart and kind and so different than what I had imagined. Whenever I'd thought of movie sets and directors before, I always thought they must be intense, drive fancy cars, and boss everyone around in order to get what they wanted. Mr. Fenway and his wife Gina were different and I wanted to understand why.

I closed my eyes as Mr. Fenway prayed,

"Dear God, we are so grateful to you. Thank you for the gifts and talents that you have given us. You always know what is best and we thank you. God, we know we cannot do anything without your help. So I pray for each person that is part of making this movie. I pray that their relationship with you grows over this summer and that they would see and understand your love for them. Be with us today and for the weeks ahead. Amen."

"Amen," I said quietly, and in my heart I knew that I wanted exactly what Mr. Fenway had prayed for me. I wanted to understand God's love the way that he did.

I opened my eyes and spotted Mallory flouncing through my new circle of friends from across the room. She was chipper as always. Her arms were wide open and she was headed in my direction.

"Good morning, Kay B and Lena!" She scooped us in close with one big motion.

"Hey, Mallory!" Kay B easily matched her enthusiasm. "Let's get you ladies to hair and makeup and get this day started!"

As we trotted off towards our designated places, Mom called for my attention, "Did you get enough to eat, Lena?"

"Yes, ma'am!" I turned to reply. Kay B gave Mom a thumbs up and we continued on our way.

My brain was full of so many thoughts but I tried to focus on what was next.

"So Lena, what do you think about this whole movie thing now that you are here? I love that Mr. Fenway cares so much about the people that work with him." Mallory settled into her chair and waited for the makeup team to get started.

I took my seat next to her and thought carefully before answering. It was hard to believe that I'd made it through my first week of making a movie. I had to admit that it wasn't nearly as scary or as hard as I thought it would be. It actually wasn't anything like I thought it would be. No one treated me like I didn't know what I was doing, no one expected me to do everything right, and no one seemed to have all the answers. It felt like I was a part of one big family and we all needed each other in order for the day to work.

I didn't think she wanted to hear everything I was really thinking, so I gave her a quick smile and said, "I'm really enjoying it! I like him and Gina a lot . . . it's like . . . I want to be like them when I grow up!"

Mallory laughed, "That's great! But why wait? You can be like them now, ya know? You kind of already are."

"What do you mean?" I asked.

"I mean did you ever think that God would do this? Take a dream you had about something you wanted and do something so much bigger and amazing with it! I think so many people's lives will be changed by this movie! Just like the Fenways had a dream and now look . . . here we are."

I sat very still for moment. I didn't know if I should tell Mallory that this movie thing actually hadn't ever been my dream.

"Lena, the same way God helped make the Fenways' dream come true by guiding them to making movies is the same thing God is doing for each of us. You don't have to wait 'til you're grown up. . . . God's using you now through this movie."

"Wow, I never really thought about it that way. Can I tell you something, Mallory?"

"Yup," Mallory answered without hesitating.

"I never actually had a dream to be in a movie. I had never even thought about it before you posted your video."

"Wow! So what made you want to audition then?"

"Well . . . I really just wanted to meet you."

Now I felt silly.

"Lena! I love that! God knows things that we don't. So sometimes He uses the things we like or love in order to make His plans happen! So you thought you just wanted to meet me, but God wanted people to meet Him through you."

"Wow. That's so weird to think about. I'm just happy I am getting to learn from Mr. Fenway and Gina and you and everyone else. Last week I was so scared that I almost didn't come. But now I am so glad I didn't let that stop me. I'm really glad I'm here."

"Aww, me too!" Mallory replied with an air hug but kept her eyes open and looking directly at me. I felt weird and I needed to say something to distract her sentimental stare.

"Sooooo, my dad and my sisters come tonight," I blurted out randomly.

"Aww, yay! That's great! I can't wait to meet them— I'm sure they are awesome just like you!"

"Lena?" Kay B called out. "They just called for you. Are you ready?"

Phew! I guess it was good that the hair and makeup people were great at what they do and could do their jobs while we chatted about things like dreams and stuff.

Mr. Fenway walked into the room and hustled over to our chairs. He stooped down until we were eye level.

"Lena, today we are going to shoot the scene where you meet Mallory for the first time. You are at the hospital. Remember, you are really sad and feeling lonely. Your family just received the news about your grandmother's illness."

"Ok," I said.

He turned and looked at Mallory. "You'll be shooting another scene next door. Gina has a team over there and will give your directions. Head on over when you are finished here."

None of what Mr. Fenway said made any sense to me but Mallory nodded and so did I.

I followed him to the area where we would be filming. It was a large empty room with three rectangular tables sitting in the middle. Each table had a tiny clear vase each with one white-pedaled flower. There were about eight chairs at each table and they were all empty. Mr. Fenway pointed to the one he wanted me to sit in. There was the usual group of crewmembers hurrying around to set up the lights and cameras and everyone was acting normal but I was confused. I glanced down at my sides to make sure I knew what scene Mr. Fenway was preparing for.

Just as he had explained, the paper read: *"Natalie meets Jennifer for the first time."*

"But why is Mallory headed to film next door?"

Normally I don't ask him a lot of questions but I had to know how this was going to work. I could not possibly film a scene with Mallory, without Mallory being there.

"Oh, good question!" Mr. Fenway chuckled and I exhaled. "We will film her portion of this scene later on today. We are just going to get a few close shots of you. You will be pretending to talk to her. You know when you watch a show and two characters are sitting close and talking but you only see one?"

I nodded.

"Well, this is how they do it. We can get more done in less time if, while we film your close ups, we have Mallory filming another one of her scenes somewhere else. Instead of having her just sit here and watch."

"Ohhhhh, I see!"

"Perfect. Now let's get going. As soon as I say action, I want you to say your first line and look up. That way it will look as though Mallory is just walking over to the table. Got it?"

As soon as he finished, he stood up and stepped away. I sat up straight in my chair and looked straight up just like he'd told me. Out of the corner of my eye, I could see the camera gliding closer to my face. My eyes really wanted to move but I remembered to never look at the camera.

I repeated my line, "I can't believe this is happening," and waited for my next instructions.

"Cut!" I heard Mr. Fenway yell, then I saw him whisper

to the man holding the really long stick with a dangling light over my head.

The light wiggled a bit when the man shifted from his left foot to his right, inched forward a smidgen, and then found his balance once again.

We repeated this scene for the next hour until finally the microphone, the light, my pretend stare, and the invisible Mallory all worked together perfectly.

I was so relieved to hear Mr. Fenway finally yell, "We got it!"

"Lena, good work! You are free for about an hour or so! Your movie mom and dad will be on set today and we will film your first scene with them. Then call it a day. Stay close. Kay B will grab you when we're ready."

"Perfect!"

I raced off and headed back to the hair and makeup room. I was hoping Mallory was back but she wasn't.

I twiddled my thumbs, looked around the empty room, and considered my options. My little black book peaked through the open zipper of my book bag so I pulled it out, found a comfy corner, and decided I needed to go ahead and empty my brain. I'd learned so much in the last three hours and if I didn't write it down, I was sure I would forget it.

Hello there, Stars!

I am feeling really good today! I'm so glad God gave me this opportunity. So far it's been really great.

*I'm glad I decided to come and be a part of it. Mr.
Fenway is so nice! I am glad he's not mean and
bossy like I had thought he would be. I would be
absolutely, positively MISERABLE if he was.*

*God, you really do know what you are
doing! Even when I don't understand
exactly what's going on, you always have
it under control. It's kind of like filming
a scene with Mallory without her being
there. I can't see the whole picture now but
later on when Mr. Fenway puts everything
together it will be great. I think that's what
my life is like—once you put all the pieces
together it will be great!*

*I could get used to this making a movie
thing!*

Chapter 12

"Lena, Lena, Lena."

I knew someone was calling my name but I was in that awkward space between being slightly awake but still dreaming too. I could not tell if it was a baby squirrel's voice or an actual person that I heard until I felt the pressure of a tiny little body easing its way next to mine.

"Lena, can I sleep with you?"

It was Ashton.

Even with my eyes practically shut, I could see that the little purple hand on my alarm clock was pretty close to the seven. Ashton had only beat my alarm by a few minutes.

I rolled over and welcomed her in. Of course Amber was just a few steps behind and inserted herself right between me and Ashton. We shuffled a few blankets around and tried to get comfortable.

Ansley heard the commotion and in a matter of seconds we were all wide awake. It had been a long weekend with touring our new city and filling Dad in on everything I had already done. I needed to be on set in just a few hours and didn't want to be awake yet. I remembered how lonely the room felt before my sisters got here so now that they were, I was excited to spend time with them.

"Guys," I started, "I have to get up in a few minutes anyway."

"So Lena, what do you do there all day anyway?"

Ansley made her way across the room, jumped up into my bed, and landed on my ankles.

"Hmmmm, well let's see . . . as soon as I get there Kay B meets me at the door. You guys met her at dinner on Saturday. She is the really funny one with the pink hair. She tells me what to do, but not in a mean way. Mr. Fenway is like the big boss but Kay B is in charge of getting me places and making sure I'm on time and know what to do."

Once I started talking I couldn't stop. "There are so many people around. You can't really see them when we're filming but there are people holding the lights, and doing all sorts of things with the sound. I wear a little microphone on my waist. It looks cool but it's actually a little annoying when I have to use the restroom . . ."

"And guys," I kept going, "there is a whole rack of clothes that they bought just for me! We call that wardrobe. So as soon as I get on set Kay B takes me to wardrobe." I paused. "Well actually, no, she normally takes me to hair and makeup.

"Did you know I get to wear makeup? They put a clear powder on my face, something shiny on my eyebrows, and they always make sure my lips match my shirt! That part's so fun!"

"Lena . . ."

"One sec, Ashton. When I first get there we have a meeting but it's sort of like a devotional time too. We stand in a circle and hold hands just like Dad does with us at home!"

"Aww, that's so fun. When I'm your age, can I be in a movie too?" Ansley crawled up my legs until we were face-to-face.

"Yup! Just talk to God about it. He has fun stuff planned for you too!"

"Like you did?" Amber asked.

"Uh, yeah. But I don't think I did a good job at first."

"You can't do a bad job talking to God, can you?" Amber's question made me think.

I wasn't sure how to answer.

"Let's ask Dad later," I said. "Right now I want you to tell me about school last week! What did I miss?"

Amber, Ashton, and Ansley started describing every detail that I'd missed. I was surprised when she said that Ms. Blount had asked about me and told them to tell me to have a great time. I didn't even think she would notice I was gone. Hearing that she did made my heart happier than I wanted to admit.

When Ansley started telling me about the chicks I laughed until my stomach hurt. She explained how they escaped again and ended up in the hall! She even got out of bed and pretended to be Mr. Lipscomb, running down the hall chasing them. I wished so badly that I could have seen that. Amber added that on the very last day, Mr. Lipscomb announced that this summer he was going to build a chicken coop outside for them since they were getting too big for his classroom. He was also starting a program to give the eggs away to families who needed them.

I closed my eyes and pretended I was there. The longer I laughed and listened, the more my mind started to think that maybe being away wasn't as exciting as it had seemed. My sisters were having so much fun sharing their memories that I didn't want to interrupt them but I was doing my best to keep smiling. The tears were starting to well up in my eyes and I tried hard to make them stop. I missed being home.

My little alarm clock started buzzing. I needed to get up and get ready for the day.

I hopped out of bed and left Ansley, Amber, and Ashley to continue their conversation without me. They didn't even seem to notice I'd left.

My morning routine had become quite simple. I'd figured out a way to get ready in just a matter of minutes. I brushed my teeth, pulled my hair into a big bun, and threw on a pair of gym shorts, a T-shirt, and blue and silver flip flops.

"Ready!" I announced.

Dad met me in the kitchen with a smile. "So Lena, this is fun, huh? You don't have to do anything in the morning, not even eat! They take care of all that for you now that you're a big star!"

I fell into Dad's arms and laughed. It was true, they did take care of me. But I definitely did not feel like a big star.

"Have you seen that car, Daddy?" I asked while trying to hold back the laughter. "Would they make a big star drive that?"

Dad laughed until his body folded in half. He could barely breathe and I didn't blame him. Even after driving around in it for a week, I still thought it was just as hideous as the first day I saw it.

Slowly everyone trickled into the kitchen and I was reminded of Amber's question. I wasn't sure what Scripture Dad was going to read to us this morning, but now was the perfect time to ask him about talking to God.

"Daddy, you know how I had prayed about being in this movie but then I still cried and worried a lot?"

"Yes . . ."

"Does that mean I did a bad job of talking to God?"

"Oh no, baby! You can never do a bad job when you talk to God!"

Dad reached across the counter top for his black Bible. He opened it, flipped a few pages, and handed it to me to read.

"Read 1 Chronicles 16:11 to us."

"Seek the Lord and his strength; seek his presence continually." I read the words out loud and then said it once again, in my head. This verse didn't say anything about prayer so I wasn't sure he had understood the question.

"Without God, we do a bad job at everything. So God wants us to seek Him, to talk to Him about everything! He doesn't expect us to have and do everything right, without Him. So no, you did not do a bad job. You did the right thing by seeking Him even when you didn't understand everything. A bad job would be not talking to God at all."

Watching Dad talk to us reminded me of Mr. Fenway. Dad had the same look in his eyes and even though there were four of us plus Mom, it always seemed like his eyes and attention were on each of us equally.

Dad squatted in front of us and spoke softly, "Girls, I never want you to think that you have to figure things out on your own. You can't make the right decisions, choose the right friends, and fix your life all by yourself, ok? Mommy and Daddy are here, but even more than that, God is here.

Ask Him for help and keep Him close in your heart—seek Him. Ok?"

"Ok, Daddy." Ashton looked around briefly before blurting out, "Can we eat now?"

"Of course." Dad smiled. He stood up straight and gently tapped Ashton on top of her head. Mom and I hugged everyone and left.

For most of the ride I thought about everything my sisters had reminded me that I missed. I had been so busy learning everything I needed to know for the summer that I had not even had a chance to think about school, the awards banquet, or anything else.

I remembered how I'd been counting down to summer and now none of it even mattered. I thought about maybe counting down til school starts but thankfully that thought didn't last long. I wasn't ready for school but I definitely wanted home. I missed Emma and Savannah.

For the rest of the day, I couldn't help but let my thoughts wander.

I even told Kay B how I was feeling. I didn't really think she would even hear me. She was actually listening for my cue as we stood face-to-face in a tiny hallway with red walls and no windows behind one of the biggest cameras I'd ever seen. I was needed on set in just a few minutes.

While we waited I whispered, "I really miss my friends."

I was a little surprised when she responded, "Lena, you'll see them soon. Just a few more weeks. And you have lots of new friends here now too!"

She was right. I did have lots of new friends, but that did not stop me from missing my other ones.

I was starting to think that no matter how great things got, I would always miss my old life.

Dear Stars,

Why did I even bother to tell Kay B how I felt? I knew she wouldn't understand.

She and Mallory are always so chipper and excited. Feeling sad around them made me feel guilty. I know I'll see them soon, but seven weeks is a long time and I miss Emma and Savannah. That doesn't mean that I don't like the people here though, does it?

God, can you make the time go by a little faster? And can you help me not to be miserable when I think of home, but to be happy with all the new friends and people I am meeting? Thanks.

Chapter 13

"We're halfway there!"

I gasped. I could not believe my ears when Mr. Fenway made this announcement in our morning meeting.

I'm not sure how God did it but it really felt like the time was going by fast. I'd filmed on a playground, in two different homes, and even in a car with a camera attached to it while driving on the highway! I'd also started helping some of the crewmembers with collecting lightbulbs, finding props, and adjusting the sound. Every day was a new adventure and I'd learned a lot about making movies and new friends.

This week we were filming in an actual hospital and things were starting to feel a little different.

I could tell Mr. Fenway was trying to sound encouraging but his voice was raspier than normal and his eyes looked tired.

This week was hard.

We'd gotten to the part in the movie where my movie family has to deal with really sad news and the characters are just starting to seek God more in their lives. Mr. Fenway asked everyone on set to pray that what was happening in the movie would also happen to the people who watched it in real life.

I had been praying for that every night. For everyone that watched the movie and even for myself.

Even though everyone was acting, four long days with no laughter and forced tears were affecting the usual level of enthusiasm on our team. I was ready for the weekend.

Kay B could tell that I was getting a little bored with all the serious and sad scenes so she tried to find different ways to keep me entertained. She taught me new card games, we explored the building together, and ventured outside to the food trucks that were located outside of the hospital. Whenever I wasn't needed, Kay B would sneak me out to grab some yummy snacks.

When Mr. Fenway finally yelled, "Cut! We got it!" today, no one cheered louder than me.

I headed straight to my dressing room, removed all of my jewelry, and switched out of my movie clothes before Kay B could even catch up.

"See ya tomorrow, Kay!" I called as I whisked past her and headed out the door to meet Mom.

On the short ride home, in our little spaceship wagon, Mom and I discussed the day. I did most of the talking. I told her everyone had still been really sad and quiet all day. She didn't say much but she assured me that by Monday everyone would be back to normal.

Just before we pulled up to the house she leaned over and said, "I have something that will make you happy. Someone's waiting for you tonight."

"Amber, Ansley, and Ashton?" I asked. I would love it if they were not ready for bed yet and we could get ready together.

She bit her lip like she does when she's trying to hold on to the flavor of something delicious.

"Daddy? A movie night?" I probed. Maybe he wanted to have a super fun family night! Mom kept quiet. I could see that she was determined not to say a word.

I hopped out and ran to the door as fast as I could. Ashton opened it before I could even put my hand on the doorknob. Her smile was huge and her eyes were full of anticipation. She used her pointer finger to direct my attention to her left. My surprise was waiting against the wall.

"AHHHHHH," I shrieked. I could not believe my eyes! Standing right in front of me were Savannah and Emma!

All six of our arms went flying into the air until they finally landed around each other's necks. We left them there for at least thirty seconds. Austin was barking and jumping on my waist. He was trying his best to join our reunion, but none of us wanted to let go.

"I missed you guys so much!!" I shouted.

Our arms fell to our sides but our hands all linked with one another's. Huddled together, hand in hand, we skipped into the living room.

It felt so strange. So exciting. So normal. I sat quietly for a few seconds and just stared at them both. Having my friends here felt like a dream and I was waiting for someone to pinch me! Austin must have read my mind, because he charged toward us, jumped up on my lap, and nibbled on my kneecaps.

"Ouch, Austin!"

Emma and Savannah looked the same but darker. I knew they were just returning from Savannah's family vacation in Mexico, the vacation I was supposed to have been on with them. Savannah's skin had turned from its normal golden color to a dark summer bronze glow. She had her curly sand-colored hair pulled back behind a white headband, to match her white tank top and blue volleyball shorts. Unlike Emma, Savannah always matched.

Emma was wearing a pair of old jeans that she'd cut and created shorts from last summer, with her purple and white striped knee socks, a neon orange T-shirt with a huge yellow emoji wearing glasses and the word "nerd" plastered across the middle. She had one long hot-pink braid cascading from the top of her head down to her shoulder. "Mexico?" I said.

"Yup." She shifted her eyes quickly. I knew she was trying to be sensitive to my feelings. Missing Mexico was definitely a bummer for me.

"Guys, we have so much to talk about!" Savannah interrupted as she pulled her knees up tighter and curled up on the couch between us. I reached behind our heads and pulled down a small cream blanket and tossed it over our legs.

Austin bounced from my knees to my friends' and back again. I felt a smile creep across my face. I may have missed Mexico but at least now we were all together. I knew I missed Emma's craziness and Savannah's ability to make sense out of it, but sitting with our knees practically on top of each other, made me realize just how much.

"So Lena, how's it feel to be a movie star? Are you and Mallory like best friends now?" Emma picked up on Savannah's attempt to shift the conversation and decided to help.

"Oh no, I'm not a movie star. Mallory is great though.

You will like her. But I don't want to talk about that right now."

"LENA! We have to! I want to know what it's like. Do you have a fancy dressing room with a big gold star and your name sketched across the door?"

I sat silently and let Savannah continue.

"Ooooh, I bet you will start getting fan mail and gifts from strangers who want your autograph! Lena, pretty soon you will need a bodyguard!"

Once Emma finished describing what she thought my life had become, she and Savannah gawked at me and waited for some sort of confirmation that Emma was on the right track. I sat quietly, refusing to participate. I tilted my head down and shook it from side to side. I didn't want to talk about the movie. I wanted to pretend that we were back in Texas and had spent the last four weeks swimming, hanging out at each other's houses, watching hours and hours of our favorite shows while dancing around in our socks during the commercial breaks.

"Girls!"

I was glad to hear Mom's voice.

"It's already been a long day for everyone, so before you get too comfortable, take your showers and put your PJ's on. That way you can talk for the rest of the evening until bedtime!" Mom poked her head from behind the way leading to the kitchen. "You will have all weekend to catch up and giggle!" she added.

I was ready to switch topics but I didn't want to move. But I also knew Mom was right. Once we started talking it would be hard to get us to stop. We all jumped up together.

I headed toward my bedroom and Savannah and Emma went toward the guest room. I heard Ashton and Amber follow them.

"Leave them alone so they can get changed, guys!" I shouted playfully even though I knew they wouldn't listen. Emma and Savannah are like sisters to them too. "Let's hurry!"

About seven minutes later we were all mostly dressed the exact same way—colorful, fuzzy socks, big T-shirts, and gym shorts. This had been our sleepover uniform since the third grade and we each happily embraced it.

We returned to the living room and helped Mom set bowls of popcorn, chocolate pretzels, Skittles, and drinks on the little table in front of the TV. I had eaten dinner on set before shooting the last scene and Emma and Savannah had eaten on their flight. Mom said the snacks were just for fun.

Ansley, Ashton, and Amber begged to stay up with us. Mom agreed that they could as long as they didn't get too hyper from the candy. I didn't think it was a good idea but I was way too happy to ruin it for everyone else.

We each found our perfect spot on the couch. Of course, Austin plopped himself directly between our feet and the table. He watched carefully and followed our fingers with his nose as we grabbed handfuls of snacks. He was hoping to catch an occasional kernel or a crumb. After a few seconds of disappointment, I watched as he leaned back on all four of his paws and pounced toward the table at full speed.

"Austin!" I screamed as he landed with one paw planted

right in the middle of the bowl of rainbow-colored candies. Amber jumped up and tried to grab him just as he dove nose-first for the chocolate.

We all watched as he escaped her grasp and darted to the other end of the table, wiggled his bottom from side-to-side, and jumped off. Skittles and popcorn scattered everywhere and Austin landed flat on his belly and stayed put as if his failed table attack had never happened.

Suddenly, we all started laughing hysterically at the scene in front of us. Amber stood over Austin with one hand on each hip attempting to correct him. "No, Austin!" she shouted. Austin raised his head briefly, turned, and flopped back down on the other side.

"Lena, the runaway chicks must have taught Austin their moves," Emma said and we laughed even harder.

"Emma, why don't you show us your new tricks? You know, the ones you learned in volleyball camp!" Savannah teased.

Emma's cheeks turned a deep shade of red. She smiled big and jumped to her feet. "Savannah!" she shouted, pretending to be upset.

"Ohhh, show me! Show me!" I begged.

Suddenly Emma was pretending to hit a ball with the back side of her wrist and shuffling her feet awkwardly across the middle of the floor, dodging the table and the TV. She could barely control her own laughter and we couldn't help but join her. I laughed until tears formed in my eyes and the muscles in my belly started to ache. "You've almost got it, Emma!" Savannah encouraged her.

Emma stopped moving and tried to catch her breath.

"Savannah, maybe you can train me now that you are on the Huskies!"

"You made the team!" I cheered. The Huskies were a special volleyball team that you had to be invited to play with. Savannah had been wanting to play with them for two years so I was really happy to know she'd made it.

Emma returned to her cozy spot and let out a sigh. "We've missed you, Lena!"

I smiled and leaned forward. "Ok, what else have I missed? Tell me everything!"

I listened to every single word and watched every hand gesture, smile, and eye roll. I may have been missing the entire summer with my friends but I was determined to not feel like an outsider. As they talked about home, I pretended I was there the same way I had when my sisters told me about Mr. Lipscomb and the chicks. I loved the way it felt.

I was just getting ready to hear all about Mexico when Mom came running into the room with Dad just footsteps behind her.

"Lena, Lena! Mr. Fenway just called! Turn on channel nine! Remember the interview you did last week? They are showing it now!"

Dad grabbed the remote and started flipping through the channels. He found channel nine just in time to see my face, along with Mallory's, plastered all over the screen.

I was mortified. My legs started to tremble. My sweaty palms were shaking and my skin felt like it was on fire. Everything in my stomach gathered into one large lump and I thought I was going to be sick.

It was just so big—my face. I had to look closer to make sure it was really me.

Unfortunately it really was me and from that moment on, I felt like I'd lost my friends all over again.

Savannah screamed, Emma jumped up and started spinning in her polka-dot socks, and even Austin began barking uncontrollably. Dad pulled out his phone and started recording the interview, the scene that was taking place in our home, and himself. Mom started texting all of her friends.

It was complete chaos.

"Guys! Guys, please stop," I begged. "It's really not that big of a deal."

"Lena! Yes, it is!" Emma reached down and attempted to pull me off the couch.

"Guys, be quiet! They are talking about Lena now!" Ansley shouted.

Everyone immediately stopped jumping, dancing, and talking and glued their eyes to the television screen.

They were so focused on what I was saying on the screen that they didn't even notice when I slipped out of the room.

I was so disappointed. I finally had my friends with me and for a little while it felt like nothing had changed. I thought God had answered every part of my prayer. My old life had been back for a few moments and now it was gone again.

Hello, God,

Uhhh, this movie keeps changing everything. I was so happy to see my friends but now that they are here all they want to talk about is the movie! Actually, it seems like you're the only one that doesn't care whether I talk about the movie! It's taking over my life! It's all everyone has talked about for four weeks now. I need a break.

God, I know you are the one who put me here and I know that I am supposed to have crazy faith like Peter. I'm supposed to trust your plan like you told the Israelites in Jeremiah to do, and I'm supposed to see you in everything. But right now I just want to be normal. If this is how people are going to treat me from now on, then I don't want it anymore. I want my friends back and I want to just be normal. I just want to be Lena.

Chapter 14

"Rise and shine, sleepyheads," Dad's voice from the hallway startled me. Before I even opened my eyes, I could feel my cheek resting on the carpet.

"Great." I opened my eyes and looked around. First, I spotted Savannah's long slender fingers hanging off the edge of the bed. She was completely stretched out across the mattress.

Then I saw Emma balled up tightly on the other bed, under the lime green fleece blanket she bought for her flight. I was in the middle of the two beds, on the floor.

"Good thing Mom put two beds in this guest room," I said while rising up to my knees and placing a hand on each of my thighs.

Dad was standing in the doorway motioning for me to come out quietly.

I looked around and shook my head to try to wake up faster. I knew I'd come in here last night to apologize to my friends for leaving during the interview, but I was pretty sure I walked to my room before they fell asleep.

"Maybe I was just dreaming," I thought to myself.

I stepped out into the hall and wrapped both my arms around Dad's waist.

"Hi, beautiful," he said.

I stood there for a while, resting my head at the bottom of his chest.

Dad held tight for a second then gently pushed me forward so that he could see my face. "Are you alright?" He spoke just a little louder than a whisper.

"Yup!" I tried to smile big to make sure he believed me.

"Ok, well let's get you dressed. You are filming downtown at the bank today. It's a really big building and can be a little confusing. They are picking you up to make sure you get where you need to be on time."

"What about Emma and Savannah?" I interjected.

"Mom and I will bring them to the set later on this afternoon—around lunchtime," he continued. "You have about twenty minutes to get ready. Want me to fix you an egg?"

"No, I'll eat when I get there," I answered while heading to my room to get ready for the day.

Dad knows that my absolute favorite thing to do while on set is to eat, so he was probably just asking about breakfast to be nice. He was probably still worried about me after last night. I really did let my emotions get the best of me. So I was determined to make today better.

Having Emma and Savannah come to the movie set later in the day was going to be perfect. I'd have plenty of time to plan a great afternoon for us. I knew I wouldn't have a lot of free time but I already had a few ideas. I wanted to make sure they met Mallory, Kay B, and the other interns so they could see just how normal everyone is. I knew they would want to see the cameras and movie set, so I'd take them to do that right away. Mostly I just wanted to find the perfect spot for us to just hang out. I still needed to hear about Mexico!

I grabbed my iPod and found Mallory's station. I hopped in the shower, then brushed my teeth, and tossed on a pair of black gym shorts, an old yellow volleyball shirt, and Mallory's white hat with the turquoise '2' on it.

I was walking out of my bedroom just as Ashton was coming in. "Lena, you look funny," she said.

"I don't care," I said a bit snarky. "We are all wearing gym shorts today."

"Me too?" Ashton asked.

"Nope, just my friends and me!"

I poked her in the belly and stuck out my tongue.

She did the same, and with an equal amount of snark she replied, "So!"

"Lena, come on. They are here!" Dad called from the front door.

I raced down the hall, scooping up Austin on the way. His wrinkled gray paw flopped up and down as I ran. I dropped him at the front door and blew him a kiss.

"Oh, we forgot to pray!" Dad held my hands in his and said, *"Lord, thank you for Lena. Thank you for this day. Keep her safe and use her for your work today. Amen."* Then he nudged me out the door.

"Bye, Daddy," I yelled as I hopped in the back seat of the black car that was sitting outside of my house.

It took us a lot longer than usual to get to the set. I could hear the driver on the phone letting someone know that traffic was bad.

Dad was right. The big office building downtown was confusing but as usual, Kay B met me at the door where the car dropped me off. In her usual speedy fashion, she guided me down one hallway, then another hallway, and into an elevator. We finally reached the tiny room where hair, makeup, and wardrobe were waiting for me. I could tell the room was normally someone's office. There was a desk behind a big black curtain that hung from the ceiling. I was trying to see the pictures sitting in the corner when Mallory stepped down from the hair chair with "X" legs and said, "Hey, Lena-girl, you're up next!"

"Nice hat, by the way." She flicked the brim and smiled. I accidently let out a snort and said, "Thanks!"

"Oh, Mallory," I called before she left the room.

"What's up?" she turned back toward me.

"Do you remember the video I sent you? And I mentioned my two friends, Emma and Savannah?"

"Oh yeah, of course. The ones who told you about the audition, right?" she asked.

"Yup . . . well, they are here visiting me and are coming to set today and they can't wait to meet you!"

"That's awesome! Make sure you find me when they get here. Can't wait to meet them!"

Yes, I thought. I was already feeling accomplished, making plans for me and the girls.

The rest of the morning went really fast. After hair and makeup, I stuck to my normal routine—wardrobe, breakfast, mirror check with Kay B, back to hair and makeup to remove traces of breakfast from my face and fix any smudges. I also ran my lines for the day over and over again. We could finally be happy again and everyone was getting back to their chipper selves on set since the more emotional and sad scenes were done. Even Mr. Fenway looked relieved.

I really prayed we could get through the scenes much faster than normal. But we didn't. So after three long hours of filming, it was finally time for lunch. Just as I'd hoped, Emma and Savannah were waiting for me in the lunch area, wearing their gym shorts, old volleyball shirts, and baseball caps.

Mom, Dad, and my sisters were standing in a corner talking to Mr. Fenway. I am not sure what they were talking about but it looked interesting. Mr. Fenway's hands were waving through the air and Mom had her bottom lipped tucked under her top two teeth like she does when she's using all of her energy to listen. Even Ansley, Amber, and Ashton were gazing straight at Mr. Fenway's moving mouth.

Emma and Savannah were sitting at a small circular table away from everyone else. I headed straight toward them and did my best to avoid making eye contact with Mom, Dad, or my sisters. I just wanted to see my friends.

"Hi, girls!" the closer I got to them, the more excited I felt.

"Lena!" Emma greeted me.

"This building is so cool!" she exclaimed. Savannah stood up next to her, nodding and smiling.

"I know, right?" I said while motioning for them to follow me. "I've been waiting for you guys all morning!"

I looked in my mother's direction and tried to get her attention. She was still fully engaged with Mr. Fenway and I didn't want to interrupt.

Then I lowered my voice to a raspy whisper, "Come on. Let's get out of here!"

"But Lena, where are we going?" Savannah asked cautiously, without moving.

"Just around . . . it's fine. Let's go!" I said convincingly.

"Where's Mallory?" Emma demanded to know before agreeing to move.

"We will find her! I promise. Let's go!"

We were trotting quietly toward the doors when Emma reached out one hand and swiped three chocolate chip cookies from the food table. "One second, guys!" she said while giggling. "We need our energy!"

"Good point!" Savannah finally gave in and joined the fun.

I led the girls down the same hallways Kay B had led me down a few hours earlier. We picked up speed with each new turn until we reached the long hallway with elevators on each side. I remembered that we went up for hair and makeup and down for filming. I wanted Emma and Savannah to see both eventually, so I decided to let them decide which one was first.

"Up or down?" I asked.

"Up," Emma responded quickly while pushing the little red circle with the up arrow on it.

We hopped on and I pushed the button for the eighteenth floor.

I could tell by the look on Savannah's face that she was worried about something. I reached out and grabbed her shoulders. Then I leaned in forward until the brims of our baseball caps were touching and said, "It's ok. Cops in LA don't arrest kids! It's against the law!"

She smirked and replied quickly, "But parents do punish them!"

She continued, "Lena, something about this just doesn't feel right." She paused, "I mean, we didn't even tell anyone where we are going."

She was right. But we didn't tell anyone because I didn't really know.

I spoke with confidence anyway, "It's not a big deal. I'm just taking you to find some of my new friends!"

"Sounds good to me!" said Emma with a mouthful of chocolate chip cookie.

When the doors opened, Mallory was standing on the other side.

Emma was so surprised and in shock I wasn't sure she was going to survive.

She started hopping up and down like a little bunny trying to reach a carrot dangling from a string.

Savannah was much more contained. She clasped her hands tightly over the middle of her chest and smiled big with her whole face.

Of course, Mallory acted like it was no big deal. She greeted them with huge hugs and even tried to guess who was who. She didn't get it right but her trying helped us to relax.

After spending a few minutes goggling at Mallory, I tried to recapture Emma and Savannah's attention.

Mallory encouraged us to have fun with the glitter and shimmery lipstick and pointed to the huge sign with an arrow and the words HAIR AND MAKEUP.

We followed the signs all the way to the little classroom

directly across from the big restroom. The door was open
and Kay B was sitting at a table eating her lunch with a few
people from the hair and makeup team.

"Hey, Lena!" she welcomed us in. "Are these the friends
you have been telling me about?"

"Yup! They are finally here—I want you to meet Emma
and Savannah!" I said gleefully.

Emma pranced right in, reached out her right hand
towards Kay B, and blurted out, "Your hair is awesome!"

Kay B jumped to her feet while extending her arms
around both Emma and Savannah at the same time. "It's so
fun to finally meet you two!"

"And I love your hair too!" she said while gently swinging Emma's hot pink braid from side to side.

"So, what are you girls going to do while you are here?
Is this your first time in California?"

"Yes!" they said in unison.

"You girls want to have some fun?" Kay B asked while
drawing our attention toward the table full of color-coded
eye shadows and an assortment of brushes and sponges.

Kay B was so easy to talk to that within a matter of
minutes she knew all about Ms. Blount, volleyball, and
Mexico. It felt like she was my big sister that my friends
were meeting for the first time.

By the time we left we were covered in hair spray, mascara, and a colorful mixture of shiny face products.

I jumped up on my tippy-toes and wrapped my arms
around Kay B's neck and squealed, "Kay B, you are the
best!" followed quickly by, "Let's go, girls!"

"Lena, you'll need to be back here for hair and makeup

in forty-five minutes. Ok?" Kay B warned as we pranced through the doors.

I turned from my waist up, winked, and gave her a bouncy thumbs up.

"Forty-five minutes, Lena!" I heard her voice chase us down the long hallway.

"Plenty of time!" I responded directly to Emma and Savannah. This was finally our chance to be alone and together again.

Emma, Savannah, and I scurried down hallway after hallway, wandering in and out of offices, peeking through windows, exploring restrooms, and waiting with anticipation behind elevator doors. We each had our iPod touches in our hands and randomly stopped for pictures along the way. We wrapped our bodies around every pole we could find, laughed uncontrollably at the strange artwork lining the walls, and listened to our voices echo throughout the large empty rooms of the forty-six-floor building.

"Here's our floor, girls!" Emma squealed, as the elevator we were on dinged at the number twenty-two.

When the elevator doors opened my jaw relaxed and my mouth drooped open. The doors faced out onto a sort of balcony that was outside, and it was beautiful. Right in front of us were the letters H-O-L-L-Y-W-O-O-D. They were boldly perched on the side of the Hollywood Hills. From this vantage point, although the sign was very far from us, each letter appeared to be within arm's reach. We were captivated by how huge and beautiful it was.

"Wow," is all we could each manage to say.

The closer we walked to the balcony's railing, the more

we could feel the California sun beating on our shoulders through our matching T-shirts. Once we reached the edge of the railing, we plopped our bodies onto the floor. Savannah laid flat on her back with her knees pointing to the sky. Emma leaned her back against the railing and stretched her legs out until they formed a perfect "V." I sat straight up between them. I could not take my eyes off the huge white letters, the hills, and city in front of us.

The three of us sat and talked. I finally heard all about Mexico and how they played with dolphins, practiced volleyball on the beach at sunset, and, of course, the braids.

I hated to interrupt our time but I knew I needed to head back to the set. I had no idea what time it was or how long we had been away. I spent so much time waiting throughout the day that I figured being a little late would not be a big deal. However, it felt like we had been gone awhile and I didn't want Kay B or anyone else to worry.

"Ok, girls. I gotta get back to work!"

We galloped toward the elevator but before we could push the button, the doors opened and Mallory was standing right in front of us. Kay B and my mother were standing directly behind her.

No one was smiling. No one was talking. No one looked happy.

"Hhhhi," I spoke cautiously. Either they had all heard about the amazing view on the twenty-second floor or I was in major trouble. I blinked quickly and prayed they were just as amazed at the big white letters as we were.

"Lena," Mom spoke first.

"What are you doing? We have been looking for you for almost two hours!" Kay B chimed in.

Before I could answer, Mallory stepped a little closer, looked me directly in my eyes, and said, "How could you do this?"

Her words froze me in my tracks.

"Uh-oh," Emma whispered.

"Shh," Savannah urged.

This was not the way I imagined our time together would end.

It felt silly and pointless to even say the words, "I'm sorry," but that's all my lips could manage to form. Mallory stared at me with disappointment for a few seconds before shaking her head and turning back toward the elevator.

"Let's go." My mother turned without looking me at me. Once Mallory removed her eyes, no one else looked at me. Not even Emma or Savannah.

"There are forty-six floors in this building and the entire crew is going from floor to floor looking for you right now. Actually, they have been looking for you for over two hours," My mother continued to talk. "Everyone spread out over the entire building, and poor Kay B even walked around outside trying to make sure you weren't hurt somewhere."

Her voice was sharp and each word pierced my heart. I knew I had let everyone down.

As I watched the numbers on top of the elevator doors count down, my heart began to beat faster and faster. By the time we reached the bottom, I could see my shirt was vibrating with each beat. I did not know who or what was waiting for me on the other side of the doors, but I knew I was in big trouble.

As the doors opened I could hear Mr. Fenway's voice. His eyes were protruding from the sockets and his nostrils were flaring. He was fuming. He glanced down at me, looked up at Kay B, and said, "Let's get her to wardrobe. We may still may be able to get a scene in."

His voice was void of its normal energetic tone and his hands were on his hips. I stood quietly and braced myself for whatever was coming next. To my surprise, he simply turned and walked away. His steps were purposeful as he made his way farther and farther down the hall.

No one was talking but I could feel the disappointment and anger in everyone's silence. I just wanted to run and hide. I glanced around quickly and considered my options.

I could feel my knees begin to wobble and my voice was weak. *"Think, Lena,"* I said in my head while trying to form some sort of explanation. But I could not come up with anything.

Without even realizing it, my legs began moving fast and I headed down the hallway in the opposite direction of Mr. Fenway.

"Lena! Did you hear Mr. Fenway? You need to get to hair and makeup now!" Kay B yelled after me.

I wanted to stop and I knew I should but I could not stop my legs from moving forward. I ran until I reached the end of the long hallway and a set of big doors.

I heard footsteps behind me so I knew someone was coming but I was too ashamed to turn and see who it was. I just wanted to get away from everyone.

Without stopping, I wrapped my hands around the large metal handles and forced myself straight through the clear doors. I ran down a narrow brick pathway and didn't stop until I found a short wooden bench to collapse on.

Seconds later the footsteps stopped and I heard a familiar voice saying, "Lena, you have to come back inside."

"I can't!" My face was planted in the palms of my hands and I cried, "Everyone hates me! I've ruined it! I knew this would happen! Asking for this was just one big mistake."

"Lena, no one hates you. Yes, we are disappointed. But no one hates you." Mallory's words were soft.

"Yes, they do!" I cried back at her. "Mr. Fenway, Kay B, my parents, you . . . probably even my friends now! Just go tell them to fire me! I never really wanted to do this anyway!" I was sobbing loudly and my breathing was quick and messy.

"Lena . . ."

"I mean it. I just want to go home! Back to my real life," I interrupted.

"Can I tell you a story?" Mallory continued without even giving me a chance to respond. Her movements were slow as she sat down next to me and reached for both of my hands. She gave them a gentle squeeze and looked me in my eyes and began, "When I was a few days old my mother noticed something different about me. Even though I was born a healthy baby, she noticed that my cry always sounded different than other babies. She said it sounded like my throat was scratched and that it looked like it hurt me to cry. She wasn't sure if it was normal so she took me to the doctor. It turned out that something was actually wrong.

After running a lot tests, the doctors told my mother that I had a rare disorder. They didn't know if I would ever be able to talk. They told my mother that I would eventually lose my voice all together."

I could not believe what Mallory was telling me. She has one of the prettiest voices I had ever heard. I picked my head up and asked, "What happened?"

"God gave me a voice." She smiled.

"You see, I know that my voice is not mine. So every time I have the opportunity to sing or speak, I am reminded that my voice and my talent are gifts from God. Using my gift is not always easy and sometimes I am really tired and just don't feel like it, but during those times I trust God to give me what I need in order to do what He has asked me to do. I know He gave me a voice so that I could share His love with everyone around me."

Mallory kept talking, "There is a verse in the Bible that says 'Whatever you do, do it enthusiastically, as something done for the Lord.' I want you to remember that verse—it's Colossians 3:23.

"See Lena, you may have just thought it would be fun to audition for this opportunity so you could meet me, but God has given you a gift. Not just in being able to act, but He has a message for people that only you can give, in your own special way. Everything about your life is God's gift and He gave it to you so that you can share His love with people too."

Mallory bent down and wrapped her arms gently around me. She squeezed me tight and said, "No one hates you. We know that you are here to use your gifts. You are not fired, but you do owe a few people an apology."

I nodded my head while still in her arms.

Then Mallory grabbed my hand and guided me back down the pathway, through the glass doors, and down the long hallway. Everyone was back to work on set and I needed to get ready. I sat in the big chair with the "X" legs, grabbed my bag, pulled out my journal, and waited patiently until Kay B was ready for me.

Dear God,

Can you help me disappear, right now⸮⸮

So many wonderful things have been happening in my life but somehow I feel so sad. I have been given an opportunity to do something so fun and even though I miss my friends and my normal life, being a part of this movie is wonderful. Instead of being sad, I need to feel blessed and grateful. How can I make myself feel that way⸮ I guess I can't. But I pray that you will change my heart.

God, are you here with me⸮ Why am I saying that when I know that you are⸮ You are always with me. So, I pray that you would forgive me for not showing you how

grateful I am and for not showing your love
to Mr. Fenway and the rest of the crew. I
haven't made the best choices. Will you
help me, today?

I still have a lot of questions about your
plans for me, but I pray that this movie will
be great. Help me to remember that people
all over the world will see this movie and
will learn about you . . . so it's really not
about me.

Amen

. . . oh no, Kay B is calling for me . . . I
have to apologize. Ohhhhh, this is so bad,
I can barely even forgive myself. What if I
apologize and everyone is still mad at me?
What if no one will forgive me?

Gotta go . . . ☹

Dear God, help me be brave!

Chapter 15

Being back on set in front of all the people I had just let down felt really weird. Actually, it felt terrible.

The words "I'm a disaster" never came out of my mouth but I felt them in my heart.

By the time the makeup crew finished covering the swelling underneath my eyes and smoothing my hair down into a neat side ponytail, my mom and dad had taken Emma and Savannah back to our house. They probably could not wait to leave.

Savannah tried to warn me about the time and Emma only wanted to make sure we had fun together. I was so ashamed and embarrassed. I wanted them to know that it wasn't their fault.

As I walked down the halls and back to set on the thirteenth floor, everyone just stared at me. Mallory stayed with me and held my hand.

She told me I needed to apologize to a lot of people and she promised that she would be right there if I needed her. I was so afraid. I would have much rather had Mallory hate me at this moment than have her show me so much kindness. I'd made so many mistakes and done really silly things ever since we met. Well, if you counted the gummy teeth, it was before we ever even met. I couldn't understand why she even still bothered with me. I wished Mr. Fenway would just fire me. That way I could go home and avoid seeing any of them ever again. But that is not what happened.

I was going to have to face everyone whether I wanted to or not.

I tried to think about what Mallory told me about herself but it wasn't really helping.

Why did I ignore the time?

Why was I so afraid that my friends would think being in a movie had changed me?

Why wasn't I as excited about this opportunity as everyone said I should be?

I could no longer tell if I was sad because I disappointed everyone or if I was simply disappointed in myself.

The first person I saw was Kay B. She was walking straight toward me. I worked really hard to avoid making eye contact with her. Mostly because my eyes were full of tears and I needed to hold them in. When I finally reached her, I took a deep breath and said, "I'm really sorry for not listening to you when you told me I only had forty-five minutes to hang with my friends."

She stooped down until we were the same height and I finished the apology I had rehearsed in my head. "Thank you for taking such good care of me. I am sorry for letting you down. Will you forgive me?"

Kay B held both of my cheeks in one hand and pinched my nose, "Of course . . . you little booger!" Her smile was big and genuine. Apologizing didn't make me feel any better but I could tell that it made her happy.

Kay B bounced away as if things were completely back to normal. I took a deep breath in and exhaled more air than I took in. I felt my chest collapse and my knees felt wobbly. Mallory rubbed her hand across my back and said, "You're ok. Good job. Keep practicing the hard things."

I stared straight ahead and said, "Hard things, like finding the people you hurt and asking them to forgive you?"

Her response was short, "Yup."

I kept walking.

The next voice I heard was Mr. Fenway calling my name, "Lena, we're ready for you."

I walked as slowly as I could to the set where he was waiting for me. My head was still hurting from all the crying I had done and the palms of my hands were wet and sticky.

"Practice. Hard things." I repeated Mallory's words in my head until I was face-to-face with Mr. Fenway.

He placed one hand on my shoulder and let out a long sigh. I stood completely still. A few moments of silence passed but it felt like an eternity. Finally he said, "Lena, do you want this?"

I gulped.

"Remember when I called to tell you all about the part?"

I mustered up enough air to answer, "Yes."

"Do you remember that I told you we prayed about who we would give this part to?"

I mumbled another, "Yes."

"So you see, we believe that you can do this. And we want you here. But after what you did today, I'm not sure that *you* want to be here."

I could feel the tears that had been gathering in my eyelashes cascading down my cheeks like a waterfall.

Mr. Fenway continued to talk, "Movies cost a lot of money and take a lot of time to make. What you did today cost us both—time and money. I am not mad, but I am disappointed and really concerned that maybe this is all too much for you. I don't want to force you to participate in something that you don't really want to be a part of. I'm worried about you."

I could feel Mr. Fenway's words piercing my heart. I kept my eyes closed while he talked and clenched my fist at my waist. I was doing my best to stand tall and hold on tight but I was losing control. My body was quivering and my face was covered in smudged mascara and wet powder.

Mallory's words were still swirling in my head. When I heard Mr. Fenway take a deep breath, I knew that it was my turn to speak.

I unclenched my fist, raised my hands to wipe my eyes, and started to speak. I blurted out, "Mr. Fenway, I am sorry."

Then I stopped talking. I had so many other things I wanted to say, but I just could not get them out. My mouth tried to form the words, but no sound followed. For now, those five words would have to do.

"I forgive you, Lena. Let's go ahead and call it a day. I don't think we can get much more done anyway." Mr. Fenway patted my shoulder three times and looked away.

"That's a wrap," he announced.

I stood still as the guy behind the cameras starting flipping buttons and wrapping up cords. A few crewmembers adjusted the lights and began collecting their equipment while the sound guy walked backwards down the ladder, carefully lowering a microphone with each step.

"Everyone works really hard. That's why they were so disappointed with me. I guess it seemed like I didn't care about anybody else," I whispered to myself.

I finally got it.

Being a part of this movie wasn't just about me. There were so many people that work really hard to get everything ready and they need me to do my part too. Even when I don't want to. I really took advantage of everyone and they probably felt like I didn't care. I had already apologized to Kay B, Mallory, and Mr. Fenway. But there were a lot of other people I needed to say sorry to.

Mostly I needed to ask God to forgive me for not being a good example of His love.

I was not sure if I had officially been dismissed, so I took a few slow steps backwards and stood still for a moment. I felt Mallory scoot behind me and slip her hand into mine. We turned slowly and walked away quietly.

I waited in my little dressing room for someone to take me home.

I picked up writing in my journal right where I had left off.

Dear God,

I still don't know if they hate me, but will you help me to make better choices? I don't want to disappoint anyone else. Especially not you, but I really need your help.

Chapter 16

When Mom poked her head into the room, she was not smiling but her face was soft and her eyes were sad. We traveled quietly through the halls and out the big glass doors. As soon as we reached the car, she stood in front of me, reached for my hand, and wrapped her arms around me. I collapsed into her chest and sobbed.

"I'm sorry. I'm sorry." I continued to cry.

I spent the entire drive home in silence, embarrassed by my choices and preparing for a long awkward evening with my friends. If they still wanted to be called that.

I walked in the house with my head down. I had no idea what Dad was going to say but I knew it wouldn't be good.

Immediately, I could smell Mom's taco soup and my ears recognized mariachi band music blasting from somewhere in the house. When I looked up Emma and Savannah were standing in the middle of the living room wearing bathing suits and large sombreros with red, yellow, and green straw intertwined through each pointy top.

The little living room table was covered in a flowery tablecloth and topped with chips, salsa, and three bowls of melted cheese.

I could not believe my eyes, nose, or my ears.

"Bienvenido a Mexico, chica!" Emma raced toward me holding a little red plastic cup with a tiny hot pink umbrella

hanging over the rim. Savannah stepped forward and placed a sombrero over my messy hair.

Ansley, Amber, and Ashton ran from the back of the house screaming and giggling.

"Welcome to Mexico, Lena!"

I reached down and hugged them all at once. Austin scurried around us trying to break into the fun. The speed of his wagging tail was doubled and he leaped in the air, landing a paw on each of my shoulders. Before I knew it, I was lying flat on my back.

"Austin!!!" we all screamed.

Just when I thought nothing could be better than this, Dad trotted down the hallway holding a pink and white volleyball.

"Anyone want to play?"

"Of course!" I squealed.

Dad opened the front door and took one step out, "Well, come on!"

"Get your bathing suit on, Lena! We don't have sand, but this is beach volleyball!" Emma could barely finish her sentence before bellowing out a deep hardy laugh.

I followed her instructions, changed quickly, and ran out front to play.

After Mom, Emma, Ashton, and I beat Dad, Savannah, Amber, and Ansley we headed back inside for dinner—taco soup!

When I thought the party was over, Emma announced that she had one more surprise. She ran to the guestroom and I could hear her rummaging through her luggage. When she returned she was holding a huge white poster behind her back.

Savannah was quiet but could barely contain her excitement. She was squirming and swaying from side to side. I had no idea what Emma was holding. I glanced at Mom and Dad to try to get a clue but they looked just as curious as I felt.

Once our anticipation reached its limit, Emma began, "So Lena, after you left we went to school and told everyone about the movie. They were all excited for you. Like everyone in the fifth grade was talking about it for the entire last week of school."

"In third grade too!" Ansley wanted to make sure we knew.

"I know, right?" Emma acknowledged Ansley and continued. "So when we found out we were coming to see you, Savannah and I wanted to find a way to let you know how we all felt. We've been waiting for a good time to do this . . ."

She moved a little closer, pulled the huge white poster from behind her back, and turned it around. It was full of my classmates' names and pictures from our year together! I spotted Mr. Lipscomb's dissection class, our field day group pictures, and even a picture of Ms. Blount—smiling! There were also drawings of little gold stars forming the word *Shine* in the middle!

"School was already out, so we tracked down as many people as we could. Sorry if we missed a few but guess who helped us?"

"OH MY!" I gasped, shouted, ran closer, and touched it.

"Ms. Blount helped us! She's like your biggest fan!"

"Guys, I can't believe this . . ." I could not find any other words to say. I walked over to each of them and gave them full-body hugs.

I could barely sit still for the rest of the night. Dad hung the poster above the fireplace and every few seconds I would run up to it and smile.

We spent the rest of the night just being together—eating and hanging out.

When my friends and I finally piled into the guestroom for the night, we dimmed the lights and within a few seconds everyone was snoring—well, everyone except me.

I just kept smiling. My eyes didn't feel sleepy and my brain was wide awake. I had so many thoughts going through my head. I knew I needed to sleep but I needed to empty my brain first. I crept out of bed, down the hall, and into my own room. With my journal in my hands, happy tears streaming down my face, I started to write everything I felt in my heart.

Dear God,

Thank you! Thank you! Thank you! What a terrible day this was, but somehow it still worked out. I think I'll actually remember this as one of the best days ever. Maybe the best days are after bad days because it's then that I see just how much I really need your help. I know what I did today wasn't right, but I am so glad that no one

hates me. You don't hate me, right? Dad
says you love me all the time and I think I
am starting to feel that. No way would this
have worked out without you. Mr. Fenway
would not have forgiven me, Mallory
would hate me, and no one would want me
around anymore. But that didn't happen
and I think it's because everyone knows
your love and helped me to see it too.
Thank you for my friends and for forgiving
me. I just feel much better now.

Chapter 17

I woke up with Ashton and Amber sitting on the edge of the bed. It was still dark outside and Emma, Savannah, and Austin were still snoring.

Ashton and Amber however were fully dressed and ready for the day. Ashton was wearing her navy blue shirt with the sparkly silver circles to match her gray glitter leggings. Amber was sitting right next to her in her pink and white polka-dot leggings, white T-shirt, and rainbow-striped rain boots.

"Why are you guys already dressed? What time is it?" I whispered.

"Hmm, I don't know," Amber said quietly while shrugging her shoulders. Ashton didn't even bother to reply. She just looked me directly in the eyes waiting to see what I would say next.

"Is it raining?" I asked.

"Nope," Amber said with a giggle.

"Well . . ." I stopped midsentence, hoping she would explain why she was wearing rain boots or why she was wearing them while sitting on the edge of the bed while it was still dark outside. But she didn't and neither did Ashton.

I dropped my face into my pillow and laughed. I could feel them still sitting there staring at me.

"Mexico was so fun, wasn't it?" Ashton asked. She looked off into the distance with a smile in her eyes.

"Yeah, it was." I grinned. "It was the best."

I flipped over on my back and looked at them. Amber just kept giggling and Ashton was playfully switching between a smirk and a grin. My heart felt full and my insides felt warm.

"Lena . . . guys . . . what are you doing?"

Ansley was awake now too.

"Nothing," Ashton informed her.

"Lena, what time do you have to leave today?" Ansley sat up and tucked her legs underneath her.

"Mmmm, I don't have to be on set until noon today," I answered. "I wonder what time it is now."

Ansley reached under her pillow and pulled out the watch she had gotten for her birthday two years ago.

"It's 5:33," she said.

Ansley squinted her eyes and asked Ashton and Amber why they were dressed. They responded with more giggles and said, "We don't know! We just wanted to play."

Ansley shook her head and so did I.

Just then Emma popped her head up. "So Lena, you are going back?"

"Back to set? I think so . . . I feel like I have to," I answered.

Emma looked at me concerned. "But you don't want to?" she asked.

I paused before answering, "Yeah, I do."

"Good." We heard another voice. Savannah was awake. I sighed.

"Before we left yesterday I heard Mr. Fenway telling your mom how much he loved working with you and that he wanted you to keep at it," Emma spoke while hopping up and into the bed with Ansley. "Plus I've already told everyone I know that my best friend is famous!"

"EMMA!!" I screeched.

Everyone started laughing and snorting. I looked around at each of them. Seeing their smiles, hearing them laugh, and knowing they were all my friends no matter what was just what I needed in order to face everyone again today.

"So Lena," Ansley said. I could tell that she was just getting started with her questions so I braced myself.

"What did you guys do while you were missing?"

Amber hurried and tried to shush her but Ansley kept talking anyway. "We were all so scared when we couldn't find you. Mr. Fenway had everyone pray that you were ok."

"He did? Well, I'm sorry about that. The whole thing was a huge mistake," I admitted.

Amber kicked her boots off to reveal her green, yellow, and white striped socks and stretched out her body right next to mine. Ashton followed her and slid her long toes from inside her soft blue ballerina slippers before curling up on the other side of me.

"I guess I just wanted to hang out with my friends like I did back home but I didn't do it the right way. I should have told someone where we were going. And I should have kept better track of the time."

Savannah nodded her head and added, "Yeah, we weren't being very responsible."

"Nope," said Emma, "but it was fun being together. Before we got in trouble, when we hung out with Mallory and Kay B. They're great."

"We miss you, Lena," Savannah said. "But we understand that you have people counting on you here. As soon as you get home we will have plenty of time to hang out. We can wait until then!"

"Yeah, I know. It's just really hard. Like suppose things are different when I get home. Like the other night when the interview came on, everyone was so focused on me on the TV that no one even paid attention to me leaving the room."

"But we are just so excited for the movie because you are in it."

"I know, Emma. It's just, well you know, I like being here and everyone is so nice. I'm learning a lot and I think I may even want to make movies one day. But sometimes it feels like this stuff is taking over my life. But maybe it is supposed to . . . I don't know."

No one spoke for a while after that. The room was silent but it felt like we all shared the same thoughts. We were friends and as I lay there surrounded by them—my best friends and my sisters—I knew that no matter what we would always be together.

My eyes were closed when I felt Ansley taping on my shoulder. "Here, Lena." When I opened my eyes I saw her birthday watch dangling from her hand. "Keep this in your pocket!"

As always, Ansley had found a way to make us all laugh. Once we settled down again, no one spoke and soon everyone was back to sleep.

The room was still dark. I rolled to my side, kissed Amber on the nose, and closed my eyes and whispered, *"God, thank you."*

Chapter 18

It had been four weeks since I last woke up on a floor, in a closet, or cuddled with a shoe. After my friends left, I'd started to feel more rested. Mom said I was finally learning to really relax. I liked the way it felt.

My eyes popped open and my entire body sprang forward like someone was pushing me up from beneath my bed.

I immediately thought Ansley was the culprit but I glanced over and saw that she was nestled comfortably in her bed.

The sun was shining so brightly into my room that I could barely open my eyes. I took one giant deep breath in and exhaled.

Today was my final day on set. I was just as nervous about it ending as I had been about it starting. I'd learned so much over the last couple of months and I wasn't really sure what life would feel like once this was all over. But I was excited to find out. I had made so many new friends, gotten a lot taller, and learned a lot about making movies and making friends.

I felt another hard push from below.

"Ouch!" I bounced forward again. "Who's under there?" I bent my body in half, leaned forward, and poked my head underneath the bed to investigate.

"Austin!" I whispered. Austin was sitting on his bottom

while spinning in small circles. I stretched my neck under the bed as far as I could in order to get a closer look at what he was doing.

When I realized he was nibbling on Ansley's yellow sandal I patted my hand on the floor three times, as hard as I could, "Oh no. Stop it, boy!"

Austin looked at me with a mix of sadness and fear. His head drooped down and he slowly backed away from the sandal.

"Good boy." I smiled to let him know that I wasn't upset with him. After all, I did understand his desire to destroy those sandals once and for all. However, Ansley was still attached to them and I knew she would not be happy if Austin ate them for breakfast.

I pulled myself back up to the top of my bed and flopped flat on my back and smiled.

My smile spread across my face and I could feel little butterflies making themselves at home in the bottom of my stomach once again. I recognized the feeling from earlier in the summer when I first learned about this adventure. And now it was almost over.

I rested for a few seconds longer and listened to see if anyone else was awake. The only thing I could hear was Ansley smacking her lips together in her sleep and tossing her head a little from side to side on her pillow.

I kicked my legs straight into the air and hopped out of bed. I yanked Ansley's blanket down from under her neck and ran straight out of our room, down the hall, and into my mom and dad's room. I leaped into the air, landed on their bed, and positioned myself right in the middle of them.

"Rise and shine, sleepyheads!" I said while wiggling deeper into the small space between them.

"Lena, girl, move over," Dad said. Mom never said a word but I knew she was awake.

"Come on, guys! It's party day! Aren't we are all going?" Mr. Fenway had told Mom and Dad that the entire family was invited to the last day of filming. We were going to celebrate after.

"Yes, go get your sisters up. We're getting up now," Dad said.

"Ok . . . Ansley, Ashton . . ." I started screaming before I was even out of their door.

"LENA!" I finally heard Mom's voice, "It's too early for that," she moaned.

I smiled and headed down the hall toward my sisters' room.

Eventually everyone was up and hustling about. Ansley and Ashton were discussing their breakfast options while Amber was sitting in the middle of the floor putting on her pink and white polka-dot socks. I was fully dressed in my jean overalls and long sleeve pink shirt with the little flowers on it. My teeth were brushed and I was ready to go.

I placed my star-shaped sunglasses on top of my head in order to hold my hair back, wrapped a blue plaid flannel around my waist in case it was chilly outside, and headed for the door. I could hear Austin rustling around behind me. "Come on, boy," I said while bending down and giving his ears a gentle swoosh. Even he was invited to celebrate with us today and I am pretty sure he knew it! I scooped him up into my arms and squatted down by the door.

I was going to miss this house. I knew it wasn't home but we had made so many memories there. I thought about the first day, when Mom and I were dropped off and it was just the two of us. I glanced at the sink where Mom was standing now and remembered bending over it as she scrubbed and pulled remaining pieces of grape flavored Yummy Gummy from my hair.

I slid back against the door with Austin snuggled in my lap and closed my eyes. I think even Austin knew it was our last day. He seemed a little sad.

"Let's go, ladies." Dad interrupted my thoughts. "I have a surprise!"

"What is it, Daddy?" Amber bounced up and down impatiently.

"If I told you, then it wouldn't be a surprise now, would it?" he responded.

"Ok. Listen up, girls. I want to read something first." Dad opened the Bible on his phone and started reading from Hebrews 11:

"Faith is what makes real the things we hope for. It is proof of what we cannot see. God was pleased with the people who lived a long time ago because they had faith like this. Faith helps us understand that God created the whole world by his command. This means that the things we see were made by something that cannot be seen.

"I'm going to skip to verse 8. But I think this one is very important for us," he said and then continued. "God called Abraham to travel to another place that he promised to give him. Abraham did not know where that other place was. But he obeyed God and started traveling because he had faith. Abraham lived in the country that God promised to give him. He lived there like a visitor who did not belong. He did this because he had faith. He lived in tents with Isaac and Jacob, who also received the same promise from God. Abraham was waiting for the city that has real foundations. He was waiting for the city that is planned and built by God."

He slid his phone back into his pocket and continued, "Girls, I know this sounds really confusing and it's probably a little hard for you to understand right now, but God has plans for our lives way past today. Think about this summer. How much fun it has been but also how challenging it has been at times for all of us. God knew every detail way before we did. That's why He asked us to have faith and trust Him."

Dad turned and looked directly at me. "Lena, I am so proud of you. You have grown a lot this summer. You have gotten much taller but I can also see God growing your heart. I know this has not been easy for you but God asked you to do something that made you uncomfortable so that He could use your life. And you let Him. That's a big deal! Now many people will be blessed by your gifts and talents."

Mom squeezed my hand.

"But girls, God's not just pleased with Lena because she's in a movie. He's pleased with each of you. We left our home and all of our friends for an entire summer. He knew that wasn't going to be comfortable or easy. But you guys did it, and you have loved each other and been kind all summer. That's a big deal too!"

Amber and Ashton giggled.

"I'm proud of each of you and I know God is smiling right now! Let's pray."

Amber interrupted him, "Daddy, can I pray?"

He nodded his head and Amber prayed, *"Dear God, thank you for my mommy, daddy, and my sisters. Thank you for letting Lena be in a movie and for all the people that are making it with her. Thank you for this house and for Austin. I pray that you keep us all safe and give us a good last day in California! Amen."*

We all repeated after her, "Amen!"

We each scurried out the door and piled into the back of the van. Mom slid into the front seat and closed the door.

"Blast off!" Mom said and began laughing hysterically.

The anticipation of Dad's surprise had us all excited. The twins would not stop giggling and Ansley was attempting to ask me all sort of random questions about her upcoming transition into the fourth grade. The summer was almost over and her brain was preparing for back-to-school. I wasn't really ready to think about it yet. I was just looking forward to being home.

Six minutes later Dad pulled up into the drive-thru window of a white shack with a big red sign that read, "DONUTS."

"I'll take two large coffees and eight glazed donuts," he said while leaning out of the spaceship wagon's window.

We all squealed. We had not had our traditional morning donut run in so long! Dad was right, this was a great surprise for us all.

I leaned forward to help him like I do at home. Even though Mom was in the car, it's my job to pass out the napkins and donuts. As I leaned closer to the front seat, I glanced to my right and saw a man standing a few steps away from our van.

He was so close I almost screamed.

He wasn't looking at us but while we waited for Dad to finish paying, I just kept staring at him. He was wearing something on his feet but they did not look like shoes and I could see his sockless feet through the large holes at the tops. His shirt was torn and his pants were a faded green with patches of dried dirt all over them. I couldn't take my eyes off him. I'd seen homeless people before but for some reason this man looked different. I wondered where he slept or if he slept at all.

"Why doesn't he have a home," I thought to myself. I wished I could help him.

I had gotten so lost in my thoughts that my dad's voice startled me, "Lena, here are the donuts." I turned quickly and grabbed the box.

My dad was waiting to drive away as I passed two hot donuts back to Ansley, two to Amber, and two to Ashton. The remaining donuts were mine but I just kept glancing at the man outside my window.

Mom followed my eyes to see what I was looking at. When she saw the man, her eyes filled with sadness and she shook her head.

I looked out the window at the man again and back down at the two donuts.

I knew what I needed to do. As hard as I tried to ignore the voice in my head, my heart would not let me. I needed to give the man in the faded, green pants my donuts. I needed to help him and donuts were all I had.

I turned away from the window to ask Mom and Dad but they were both already smiling. Mom nodded before the words ever formed. Dad pushed the button for the back window to go down.

"Excuse me, sir," I said as I held the two hot donuts out my window. He turned and reached his hands out. I think he was shy because he looked away and whispered, "Thank you." He had a sad face but I could see a smile in his eyes.

I hopped back into the backseat and took a deep breath. My brain felt all foggy and I felt weird. I think it was a combination of sadness and satisfaction. I desperately wanted my donuts but when I closed my eyes, I could picture the man's smiley eyes and his dirty pants. He needed them more than I did.

As Dad pulled out, I felt a soft tap on my shoulder. It was Ansley. "Here, Lena," she said and she handed me one of her donuts.

"Thank you," I squealed.

I slouched back in my seat and grinned.

As soon as we pulled into the parking garage of the set, I saw Kay B outside waiting for me as usual. She greeted each of us with a big hug and led the way while telling me what I could expect for the day.

"Today's a really short day. We just have one last team meeting and we need to take a few photos. After that we will have the end-of-filming party. That is going to be a lot of fun!"

She grabbed Ashton's hand and said, "There will be games and food for everyone!"

She showed Mom, Dad, and my sisters where they could wait and told them it would only be about thirty minutes before we headed to the party.

I followed Kay B to the room where we were meeting. Mr. Fenway thanked everyone for a great experience. He told us to continue to pray for the team as they finished editing and preparing the movie for theaters. The last thing he talked about was how important it was to be ready for radio interviews and television appearances.

"Remember, people may start recognizing you from the TV ads they see and articles they are reading about upcoming movies. It's a perfect opportunity for you all to talk about the movie as well as our mission. God will continue to use you if you are open to Him. Let people know this is a super special movie with a great message for everyone!" Mr. Fenway said as he wrapped up his talk.

After he finished talking, he asked us all to join hands to pray before everyone could head outside for the party.

As soon as he finished, I opened my eyes and spotted Mallory. She was doing a little dance and skipping toward me. She burst out laughing as I attempted to mimic her moves. I was really excited to talk to her. I needed to tell her about the man in the faded green pants.

"Hey, Lena!" she said while reaching out and giving me a huge hug.

"Hi! Guess what?" I hugged her back.

"What?" her eyes widened and she leaned in closer to listen.

I told her all about Dad's surprise and how excited the entire family was because it reminded us all of home. I told her about my job passing out the donuts and how this morning I could barely do it because of the sad looking man.

When I finally got to the part about giving him the donuts I could feel my eyes begin to fill with tears.

"Oh, Lena," she said. "I love hearing this and seeing how God is working on your heart!"

Her words sounded just like my dad's.

I didn't know why I was crying. They were not sad tears but they weren't happy tears either. It felt like my heart was just wide open and I could feel everything that was happening around me like I never had before. I didn't just feel like I was doing what people told me to do, but I was doing what I knew I needed to do. I could tell Mallory understood exactly what I was feeling.

She squeezed me tightly again and said, "When God tells you to do something, always say yes! The more you say yes to Him the more people will experience His love through your actions!"

In that moment I was more grateful than ever for the gifts God had given me. I was grateful that I had said yes to things that I didn't even want to do. I had needed this summer and I hadn't even known it.

I remembered when Mallory told me I was already like Mr. Fenway and Gina and I finally understood what she meant. I didn't need to wait until I was all grown up or to have a big dream or big plan in order for God to use me. All I wanted were donuts, but God used that to have me help

someone else. I prayed that man in the faded, green pants felt God's love.

When we stepped out of the back door there was a long red carpet leading out the door to where the party was set up. People were standing on both sides of it welcoming us to the celebration with clapping and shouting. I looked around and saw so many of the same faces that had welcomed me into the meeting on the first day of this movie adventure. They were no longer strangers. They were my friends.

After taking a few steps onto the carpet, Austin spotted me. He jumped down from Dad's arms, headed straight down the middle of the carpet, and leaped into the air and into my arms. Everyone laughed hysterically and cheered even louder.

I stood there for a few extra seconds and tried to take a picture with my brain. I wanted to remember everything exactly this way.

We spent the rest of the day eating, talking, dancing, and laughing until our faces hurt. Ansley summed it up perfectly when she said, "Leaving home and staying here in California was worth it since we got to come to such a great party!" Even Mr. Fenway laughed at that!

By the time we finished at the party everyone was exhausted. But there was one more leg to our journey. Our flight home. When we arrived at the airport even Austin was wiped out and didn't protest too much when Mom and Dad put him in his travel crate and we said good night to him, before boarding the plane ourselves.

"Flight attendants, please prepare for takeoff," the pilot

announced once all the passengers had taken their seats. I sat back and stared out of the tiny, oval-shaped window. It was dark outside but the sky was glowing. The stars seemed brighter than normal and as we took off from the runway they looked so close it felt like I could touch them.

"Hello, Stars . . ." I whispered.

"Lena, what did you say?" Ansley asked.

"Oh, just talking to myself." I looked at her and smiled.

Hello, Stars,

It's me again. I can't believe I am back home. Everything looks the same here. It smells a little different but I am sure that will go away soon.

I just wanted to tell you thank you. Thank you for being there for me this summer. I am not sure how I would have made it without you. It no longer feels weird to write on these pages. I think I am actually writing to God. At least it feels that way. He's the one that really helped me through this summer!

School will start in just a few days and I am not sure how busy I'll be, getting used to the sixth grade. I really don't know what will happen next but I pray that I'll be ready for it!

Good night for now, but I am sure I'll talk to you again soon.

Day Dreams and Movie Screens

Eleven-year-old Lena Daniels' summer of Hollywood starlets and movie filming alongside her favorite singer, Mallory Winston, is over. School will be back in full swing, and it seems as though life might just pick up where it left off—with volleyball games, homework, and her best friends.

But just as she begins to wonder if her summer was all just a dream, her world is turned upside down . . . again! The movie premiers, the previews seem to be splattered on every television and radio channel, and everyone knows her name. Her classmates, strangers, and even her friends are starting to treat her differently, and everywhere she turns she's being asked for an autograph, a picture, or a hug.

Lena is just figuring out how to manage her new fame at home when she finds out she's hitting the road on a two-week bus tour to further promote the film. Traveling across the country with the cast—with the surprise addition of her whole family joining them—Lena experiences adventures and challenges she never expected, while learning to step outside of her comfort zone and follow the path God has for her life. She learns that saying yes to God may not always be easy, but will take her further than she ever imagined!

Available in stores and online!

Connect with Faithgirlz!

 http://www.faithgirlz.com/

 www.facebook.com/Faithgirlz/

 www.instagram.com/zonderkidz_faithgirlz/

 twitter.com/zonderkidz?lang=en/

www.pinterest.com/zkidzfaithgirlz/

MOTOCROSS
DOUBLE-CROSS

BY JAKE MADDOX

illustrated by Sean Tiffany

text by Bob Temple

Librarian Reviewer
Chris Kreie
Media Specialist, Eden Prairie Schools, MN
MS in Information Media, St. Cloud State University, MN

Reading Consultant
Elizabeth Stedem
Educator/Consultant, Colorado Springs, CO
MA in Elementary Education, University of Denver, CO

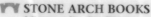

STONE ARCH BOOKS
Minneapolis   San Diego

Jake Maddox Books are published by Stone Arch Books,
A Capstone Imprint
1710 Roe Crest Drive
North Mankato, Minnesota 56003
www.capstonepub.com

Library of Congress Cataloging-in-Publication Data
Maddox, Jake.
    Motorcross Double-cross / by Jake Maddox; illustrated by Sean
Tiffany.
        p. cm. — (Impact Books. A Jake Maddox Sports Story)
        Summary: When Carlos competes against his best friend Ricky for
a place in the United States Motocross Association Nationals, each of
them thinks the other is trying to sabotage his chances at winning.
        ISBN-13: 978-1-59889-845-3 (library binding)
        ISBN-10: 1-59889-845-0 (library binding)
        ISBN-13: 978-1-59889-897-2 (paperback)
        ISBN-10: 1-59889-897-3 (paperback)
        [1. Motocross—Fiction. 2. Motorcycle racing—Fiction.
3. Competition (Psychology)—Fiction.] I. Tiffany, Sean, ill. II. Title.
PZ7.M25643Mot 2008
[Fic]—dc22   2007003636

Art Director: Heather Kindseth
Graphic Designer: Kay Fraser

Printed in China.
042015
008894R